Midwives On-Call at Christmas

*Mothers, midwives and mistletoe—
lives changing for ever at Christmas!*

Welcome to Cambridge Royal Hospital—
and to the exceptional midwives
who make up its special Maternity Unit!

They deliver tiny bundles of joy on a daily
basis, but Christmas really is a time for
miracles—as midwives Bonnie, Hope,
Jessica and Isabel are about to find out.

Amidst the drama and emotion of babies
arriving at all hours of the day and night,
these midwives still find time for some
sizzling romance under the mistletoe!

This holiday season, don't miss the festive,
heartwarming spin-off to the dazzling
Midwives On-Call continuity
from Mills & Boon Medical Romance:

A Touch of Christmas Magic
by Scarlet Wilson

Her Christmas Baby Bump
by Robin Gianna

Playboy Doc's Mistletoe Kiss
by Tina Beckett

Her Doctor's Christmas Proposal
by Louisa George

All available now!

Dear Reader,

Thank you for picking up Sean and Isabel's story.

I love being part of the Midwives-On Call at Christmas continuity series. Not only am I creating a world along with fabulous authors, but we get to meet characters over and over and come to know and love them so much more.

Isabel Delamere has a secret that involves Sean Anderson, but she knows that if he discovers it he will be out of her life for ever. She is torn between truth and lies, between the past and the present. And her feelings for Sean are complicated and bone-deep.

Small wonder, then, that when Sean turns up in her maternity unit she struggles to face him. But Sean isn't the young teenager she fell for years ago—he's a devastatingly handsome and accomplished doctor who wants answers to questions from decades ago.

I loved writing Isabel and Sean's story. It takes us on a journey from Melbourne to Cambridge and to magical Paris at Christmas time, and it gives them both a chance to rediscover love. But do they take it? You'll have to read it and see!

I really hope you enjoy reading this book. If you want to catch up with all my book news visit me at louisageorge.com. Better still, sign up for my newsletter while you're there, so you get to hear about the contests and giveaways I have too.

Happy reading!

Louisa x

HER DOCTOR'S CHRISTMAS PROPOSAL

BY
LOUISA GEORGE

First published in Great Britain 2015
By Mills & Boon, an imprint of HarperCollins*Publishers*
1 London Bridge Street, London, SE1 9GF

Large Print edition 2016

© 2015 Harlequin Books S.A.

Special thanks and acknowledgement are given to Louisa George for her contribution to the Midwives On-Call at Christmas series

ISBN: 978-0-263-26099-1

Printed and bound in Great Britain
by CPI Antony Rowe, Chippenham, Wiltshire

34757252

Having tried a variety of careers in retail, marketing and nursing, **Louisa George** is thrilled that her dream job of writing for Harlequin Mills and Boon means she now gets to go to work in her pyjamas. Louisa lives in Auckland, New Zealand, with her husband, two sons and two male cats. When not writing or reading Louisa loves to spend time with her family, enjoys traveling, and adores eating great food.

Books by Louisa George

Mills & Boon Medical Romance

One Month to Become a Mum
Waking Up With His Runaway Bride
The War Hero's Locked-Away Heart
The Last Doctor She Should Ever Date
How to Resist a Heartbreaker
200 Harley Street: The Shameless Maverick
A Baby on Her Christmas List
Tempted by Her Italian Surgeon

Visit the Author Profile page
at millsandboon.co.uk for more titles.

CHAPTER ONE

'ODDS ON IT'LL be the Pattersons. She was telling me the other day that she missed out on winning it a couple of years ago, so she's going to cross her legs until the twenty-fifth. No hot curries, or hot baths and definitely no hot sex for her.'

You and me both, girlfriend. Obstetrician Isabel Delamere tried to remember the last time she'd had anything like hot sex and came up with a blank. It was all by design, of course…working in a maternity unit was enough reminder of what hot sex could lead to—that and her own experiences. But every now and then she wondered…what the hell was she missing out on?

Plus, how could she possibly be lonely when she spent all of her waking hours surrounded by colleagues, clients and lots and lots of wriggling, screaming, gorgeous babies?

Sighing, she wrote *Patterson* down on the First

Baby of Christmas sweepstake form and added her five-pound note to the pot. 'If mum has her way there's no way that baby's coming until Christmas Day. She's set her heart on the hamper, and between you and me they don't have a lot of money. I think she needs it.'

'I admire your optimism…' Bonnie Reid, one of Isabel's favourite midwives—and new friend—at the Cambridge Royal Maternity Unit, added her contribution of a large box of chocolates and a bumper pack of newborn nappies to the crate of donations that threatened to overshadow the huge department Christmas tree and wooden Nativity scene. With a heavy bias on baby items, some gorgeous hand-knitted booties and shawls, and heaps of food staples, whoever won would be set up for the next year. 'But when I saw her yesterday that baby was fully engaged and she was having pretty regular Braxton Hicks contractions, so my bet is that baby Patterson will make a show well before Christmas Day.' Bonnie stepped back and surveyed the decorations, her lilting Scottish accent infused with wistfulness. 'Oh, I do love Christmas.'

Me too. Isabel dug deep and found a smile. Well, in reality, she loved being with her sister at Christmas; they shared a very special bond. This last year here in the UK had been the longest they'd spent apart, and the prospect of Isla doing all the traditional celebrations without her bit deep. Especially...she sighed to herself...especially when Christmas had always been so full of memories.

Isabel slammed back the sadness and tried to immerse herself in the here and now rather than thinking of her sister back in Melbourne on the other side of the world, all ripe and ready to have her first baby. She wondered whether the Melbourne Maternity Unit was taking similar bets. Maybe Isla would win the Aussie sweepstake? Now that would give the rest of the department something to giggle about: the head midwife winning with a Christmas Day baby! 'So, go on, then, who will it be?'

'Who will what be?' A deep male voice, redolent with her beloved Aussie tones. The sound of home.

The sound of heartbreak.

Isabel inhaled sharply.

Sean.

And even if the man had been mute she'd have known he was behind her simply because of the full-on reaction her body had any time he was in the vicinity. Every tiny hair stood to attention. Her heart rate escalated. Palms became sweaty. Seventeen years on and she'd managed to deal with it…when she didn't have to face him every day. She'd almost erased him from her heart.

Almost. She'd come to the other side of the world to forget him. And she'd managed quite well for close to nine months until he'd turned up, out of the blue, and those feelings had come tumbling back. The memories…and his questions… Questions she couldn't bear to answer.

Somewhere a phone rang. Somewhere voices, raised and harried, called to her. 'Dr Delamere. Please. There's been an accident…'

Oh, God. She was shaken from her reverie but her heart rate stayed too high for comfort. 'Isla?'

'Isla? No,' Bonnie called over from the nurses' station. 'Susan Patterson. Motor vehicle accident. They're bringing her in to ER. Heavy vaginal bleeding. Mum shocked. Foetal distress. ETA five minutes.'

'What? No! We were just talking about her.' Without even looking at Sean, Isabel jumped straight into doctor mode. 'Right, Bonnie, sounds like a possible abruption. Get Theatre on alert. I'll meet the ambulance down in the ER.'

'I'm coming with you.' Sean was heading towards the door.

Only when hell freezes over. 'No. Sean, absolutely not.'

Silence.

She realised that all the eyes of the staff were on her. No one knew about their history, and for as long as there was breath in her body no one was going to. 'I mean…thank you very much for your offer, Dr Anderson, but I'll be fine.'

He shrugged, following her into the corridor, into more quiet. 'I'm in a lull here. Everyone's discharged or doing well, I don't have a clinic until two o'clock. Are you really saying you couldn't use an extra pair of hands? I have done this before, you know.'

'Yes, I know.' She also knew what a talented

and empathetic obstetrician he was, she just didn't relish the prospect of spending any time with him. But she had to give this mum everything she had and an extra pair of confident hands would definitely help. 'Okay. But this is my case, my theatre, my rules.'

'Of course. If I remember rightly, it was always your rules, Isabel. Right down to the bitter end. In fact, I don't remember having any say in that at all.' He gave a wry lift of his eyebrow as they hurried towards the emergency room. 'This one time I'll abide by them. But once we're out of there then...'

She stopped short. 'Then, what?'

'Then I change the rules to suit me.'

She shrugged, hoping upon hope that he couldn't see through her recalcitrant façade to the shaking, smitten teenager she still felt like when she was around him. 'Do what you want. It won't affect me. At all.' *Liar.* It seemed as if everything he did affected her. Just being here. Breathing. In Cambridge. Goddamn him.

Isabel threw him a look that she hoped told him where exactly to shove his rules, and strode straight in to Resus. She would deal with Sean Anderson…later…never, if she had her way. 'Now, Susan? Crikey, love, what on earth has been happening?' She took hold of her patient's hand.

Mrs Patterson was lying on a trolley, tears streaming down her cheeks. Pale. Terrified. Her voice was barely audible through the oxygen mask over her nose and mouth. 'Thank God you're here, Isabel. I'm so scared. I don't want to lose this baby. Please. Do something.'

'I will. I just need some details then we'll make some decisions. And we'll be quick, I promise.' She'd have to be. If it was a placental abruption, as she suspected, both mum and bub were at serious risk. Outcomes weren't always positive. And well she knew. Too well. Isabel examined Susan's belly for the baby's position and well-being. Then she tightened an electro foetal monitor belt over the baby bump. 'Has anyone called Tony?'

'I did.' Jenny, the paramedic, filled her in on further details. 'He's on his way. Grandma's looking after the toddler. They were in the car at the time of impact. Hit from behind. Susan felt a tight pull in her belly. Possibly from an ill-fitting seat belt, but there's no visible marking or bruising on the abdomen. I have normal saline through a wide-bore IV in situ. Moderate vaginal bleeding. Blood pressure ninety over fifty and dropping. Baby's heart rate jittery and at times…' She pointed to her notes and let Isabel read. The baby's heart rate was dipping, a sign of foetal distress. Mum was clearly shocked. Judging by the blood staining her clothes the baby needed to be out. Now.

'Okay. Thanks.' Isabel turned to the ER nurse that had appeared. 'I need you to cross-match four units of packed cells. I need clotting times, usual bloods and that portable ultrasound over here as quick as you can.'

Susan's hand squeezed in Isabel's. 'But I wanted…I wanted to hang on…two more weeks….'

'I know, but these things happen and we just have to deal with them as best we can.' Isabel gave Susan a quick smile, positioned the ultrasound machine in front of her, squeezed jelly onto the probe and placed it over Susan's tummy. 'I'm just going to take a quick look.' Baby was okay—distressed, but alive. Isabel exhaled deeply. Thank God.

She looked over at Sean and saw his reassuring smile. She gave him a small one back. They both knew that at least some of the immediate anxiety was over.

But the placenta was, indeed, partially separated. The baby was at serious risk and mum's blood loss was not stopping. Despite the desperate urgency Isabel needed to be calm so as not to frighten mum too much. 'Okay, Susan, we do have a problem here, but—'

'Oh, my God. I knew it…'

'Sweetheart, we'll do our best. It'll be okay.' Isabel prayed silently that it would. 'Your placenta is failing, I think the car impact may have given it a nasty jolt or tear and there's a real risk to the baby if we don't do something soon. As you know the placenta is what keeps baby alive, so we have to take you to the operating theatre and do a Caesarean section. I need your consent—'

'Where's Susan? Susan? Where's Susan?' A burly-looking stocky man covered in dust pushed his way in, steel-capped boots leaving grubby imprints across the floor. 'What the hell's happening?'

Isabel scanned the room for Sean. But he was there already, his hand on Tony's forearm, gently slowing him down. 'Are you Tony? Here, let me bring you over. It's a lot to take in, I know, mate. There's a few tubes and lines and she looks a little pale. But she's good.'

'She is not good. Look at her.' The room filled with the smell of beer and a voice that was rough round the edges, and getting louder. 'Is that…? Is that blood? What's happened? What about my boy? The baby! Susan! Are you all right?' Then his tone turned darker, he shoved out of Sean's grip and marched up to Isabel. In her face. Angry and foul-mouthed. 'You. Do something. Why are you just standing there? Do something, damn it.'

Isabel's hand began to shake. But she would not let him intimidate her. 'I'm doing the best I can. We all are. Now, please—'

'No need for that, mate. Come away.' Sean's voice was calm but firm. At six foot one he was by far the bigger man. Broader too. And while Tony was rough and menacing, Sean was authoritative. There was no aggression, but a quietly commanded respect and attention. 'We're going to take her to Theatre right now, but first we need to know what we're dealing with. Yes? Have a few words with Susan, but then we need to get moving. I'll show you where you can wait.'

'Get your hands off me.' Tony pushed his way to the trolley. 'Susie.'

'I'll be fine, Tony. Just do as he says.' Susan started to shake. 'I love you.'

'If they don't—'

Sean stepped forward. 'As I said. Come with me. *Now.* Let's have a quiet word. Outside.' He bustled Tony out of the room.

'He's not a bad man.' Isabel's patient's voice was fading. Alarms began to blare.

'I know, I know, he's scared, is all.' Thank God Sean was able to contain him because the last thing Isabel needed was a drunk father getting in the way of saving a mother and baby. 'Now we need to get you sorted, quickly.' Isabel nodded to the porter. 'Let's go.'

She all but ran to the OR, scrubbed up and was in the operating theatre in record time. Sean, somehow, was there before her. 'So we have a crash C-section scenario. Your call, Izzy. Whatever happens, I've got your back.'

'Thank you.' And she meant it. Well drilled in dealing with emergencies, she felt competent and confident, but having someone there she knew she could rely on gave her a lift. Even if that lift involved her heart as well as her head.

Within minutes she'd tugged out a live baby boy. Floppy. Apgar of six. But, with oxygen and a little rub, the Apgar score increased to ten. As occurred with every delivery Isabel felt a familiar sting of sadness, and hope. But she didn't have time for any kind of sentimentality. One life saved wouldn't be enough for her. Placental abruption was harrowing and scary for the mother but it was high risk too. That amount of blood loss, coupled with the potential for complications, meant they were perilously close to losing her.

'Blood pressure's dropping...' The anaesthetist gave them a warning frown.

'Hang on in there...I just need to find the tear.' Isabel breathed a sigh of relief as she reached the placenta and started to remove it. 'Attagirl.'

Within an hour they'd managed to save Susan's life too, although she had hung close to the edge. Too close.

And now...well, now that dad was with baby, her patient was in recovery and the rest of the staff had scarpered, Isabel was alone. Alone, that was, with the one person she never wanted to be alone with again. Rather than look at him she stared at the words she was writing. 'Well, Sean, I don't want to keep you while I finish writing up these notes. Thanks, you were a great help. Things could have turned nasty with Tony.'

'He just needed me to explain a few things. Like how to behave in an emergency department. But I get it. The bloke was worried. I would have been too if I was losing my wife and my baby.'

Guilt crawled down her spine. How would he have been? At seventeen? Quick-mouthed and aggressive? Or the self-assured, confident man he was now? She stole a quick glance in his direction. 'You wouldn't have acted like that. So thanks for dealing with him. And for your help in here.'

'It wasn't just me. We almost lost them both, but your quick thinking and nifty work saved both their lives. Well done.' He threw his face mask into the bin, snapped his gloves off and faced her. 'You look exhausted.'

'Gee, thanks. I'm fine.' She didn't feel fine. Her legs were like jelly and her stupid heart was still pounding with its fight-or-flight response. She looked away from the notes and towards the door. Flight. Good idea. Easier to write them up in the safety of her office, which was a Sean-free zone. Snapping the folder closed, she looked up at him. 'Actually, I've got to go.'

'Wait, please.'

She stepped towards the door and tried hard to look natural instead of panicked. 'No. I have a million things to do.'

'They can wait.' His tone was urgent, determined. He was striding towards the exit now too.

'No. They can't.'

'Isabel. Stop avoiding me, goddamn it!'

He was going to ask.

He was going to ask and she was going to lie. Because lying had been the only way to forge enough distance between her and the one thing she had promised herself she could never do again: feel something.

She calculated that it would take precisely five seconds to get out of the chilly delivery room and away from his piercing blue-eyed gaze. For the last two months she'd managed to steer clear from any direct one-to-ones with him, shielding herself with colleagues or friends. But now, the things unsaid between them for almost seventeen years weighed heavily in the silence.

He was going to ask and she was going to lie. Again.

The lies were exhausting. Running was exhausting. Just as getting over Sean and that traumatic time had been. She didn't want to have to face that again. Face him again.

His scent filled the room. Sunshine. Spice. His heat, so familiar and yet not so.

Seventeen years.

God, how he'd matured into the sophisticated, beautiful man he was destined to be. But wanting answers to questions that would break her heart all over again…and his.

She made direct eye contact with the door handle and started to move towards it again.

'Izzy?'

She would not turn round. Would. Not. 'Don't call me that here. It's Isabel or Dr Delamere.'

'Hello? It's not as if anyone can hear. There's only you and me in here. It's so empty there's an echo.'

'*I* can hear.' *And I don't want to be reminded.* Although she was, every day. Every single day. Every mother, every baby. Every birth. Every stillborn. Every death.

She made it to the door. The handle was cold and smooth. Sculpted steel, just like the way she'd fashioned her heart and her backbone. Beyond the clouded glass she could make out a bustling corridor of co-workers and clients. Safety. She squeezed the handle downwards and a whoosh of air breathed over her. 'I'm sorry,

Dr Anderson, I have a ward round to get to. I'm already late. Like I said, thanks for your help back there.'

'Any time. You know that.' His hand covered hers and a shot of electricity jolted through her. He was warm. And solid. And here; of all the maternity units he could have chosen... This time it wasn't a coincidence. His voice was thick and deep and reached into her soul. 'I just want one minute, Isabel. That's all. One.'

One minute. One lifetime. It would never be enough to bridge that time gap. Certainly not if she ever told him the answer to his question.

'No, Sean, please don't ask me again.' She jabbed her foot into the doorway and pulled the door further open.

Then she made fatal error number one. She turned her head and looked up at him.

His chestnut hair was tousled from removing his surgical cap, sticking up in parts, flattened in others. Someone needed to sink their fingers in and fluff it. So not her job. Not when she was too busy trying not to look at those searching eyes. That sculptured jawline. The mouth that had given her so much pleasure almost a year ago, with one stupid, ill-thought-out stolen kiss, and…a lifetime ago. A boy turned into a man. A girl become a woman, although in truth that had happened in one night all those years ago.

Onwards went her gaze, re-familiarising herself with lines and grooves, and learning new ones. Wide solid shoulders, the only tanned guy in a fifty-mile radius, God bless the sparse Aussie ozone layer. Toned arms that clearly did more working out than lifting three-kilogram newborns.

His voice was close to her ear. 'Izzy, if it was over between us… If everything was completely finished, why the hell did you kiss me?'

Good question. Damn good question. She'd been brooding over the answer to that particular issue for the better part of the last year, ever since he'd crushed her against him in a delivery suite very similar to this one, but half a world away. It had been a feral response to a need she hadn't ever known before. A shock, seeing him again after so long, turning up at the Melbourne hospital where she'd worked. He'd been as surprised as she had, she was sure.

Then he'd kissed her. A snatched frenzied embrace that had told her his feelings for her had been rekindled after such a long time apart. And, oh, how she'd responded. Because, in all honesty, her feelings for him had never really waned.

Heat prickled through her at the mere memory. Heat and guilt. But they had to put it behind them and move forward. 'Really, Sean? Do you chase most of the women you kiss across the world? It must cost an awful lot in airfares. Still, I guess you must do well on the loyalty schemes. What do you have now, elite platinum status? Does that entitle you to fly the damn planes as well?'

His smile was slow to come, but when it did it was devastating. 'Most women aren't Isabel Delamere. And none of them kiss like you do.'

'I'm busy.'

'You're avoiding the issue.'

She held his too blue, too intense gaze. She could do this. Distract him with other issues, deflect the real one. Get him off her back once and for all. She was going away tomorrow for a few days. Hopefully everything would have blown over by the time she got back. *Like hell it would.* She could pretend that it had. She just needed some space from him. 'So let me get this straight. You turn up out of the blue at the same place I'm working in Melbourne—'

'Pure coincidence. I was as shocked as you. Pleasantly, though. Unlike your reaction.' The pressure of his thumb against the back of her hand increased a little, like a stroke, a caress.

She did not want him to caress her.

Actually she did. But that would have been fatal error number two. 'Then after I leave there you turn up here. Also out of the blue? I don't think so.'

'Aww, you missed a whole lot out…where I didn't see you or have any contact with you for many, many years. As far as I was concerned you were the one that got away. But also the one I got over.' At her glare he shrugged shoulders that were broader, stronger than she remembered. 'I put you out of my mind and did exactly what I had planned to do with my life and became a damned fine obstetrician. Then one day I turn up at my cushy new locum job at Melbourne Maternity Unit and bump into my old…flame. I never dreamt for a minute you'd be there after hearing you'd studied medicine in Sydney. I assumed you'd moved on. Like I had. But then, Delamere blood runs thick with the Yarra so I should have realized you'd be there in the bosom of your…delightful family.' He gave a sarcastic smile. Sean had never got on with her hugely successful neurosurgeon daddy and socialite mother who ran with the It crowd in Melbourne. 'Well, in that sumptuous penthouse apartment anyway. Cut to the chase—the first chance you get: wham, bam. You kiss me.'

'What?' She dragged her hand from under his and jabbed a finger at him. 'You kissed me first. It took me by surprise—it didn't mean anything.'

'No one kisses like that and doesn't mean it.'

He'd pulled her to him and she'd felt the hard outline of his body, had a crazy melting of her mind and she'd wanted to kiss him right back. Hard. Hot. And it had been the most stupid thing she'd done in a long time. Not least because it had reignited an ache she'd purged from her system. She'd purged *him* from her system. 'And now you're here to what? Taunt me? Tell me, Sean, why are you here?'

'Ask your sister.'

'Isla? Why? And how can I?' There was no way Isla would ever have told Sean what had happened. She'd promised to keep that secret for ever and Isabel trusted her implicitly. Even though over the years she had caught Isla looking at her with a sad, pitiful expression. And sure, Isabel knew she'd been badly scarred by her experiences, they both had, but she was over it. She was. She'd moved on. 'Isla is back home in Australia and I'm here. I'm hardly going to phone a heavily pregnant woman in the middle of the night just to ask why an old boyfriend is in town, am I? What did she say?'

'It was more what she didn't say that set alarm bells ringing. I asked her outright why you had suddenly gone so cold on our relationship, she said she couldn't tell me but that I should ask you myself. Between her garbled answers and your sizzling kiss, I'm guessing that there's a lot more to this than you're letting on. Something important. Something so big that you're both running scared. My brain's working overtime and I'm baffled. So tell me the truth, Isabel. Tell me the truth, then I'll go. I'll leave. Out of your life.'

Which would be a blessing and a curse. She was so conflicted she didn't know if she never wanted to set eyes on him again or...wake up every morning in his arms. But if he ever found out why they'd split up option two would never, ever happen. He'd make sure of it. 'It doesn't matter any more, Sean. It was such a long time ago.'

'It matters to me. It clearly still matters to Isla, so I'm sure it matters to you.' He leaned closer and her senses slammed into overdrive. Memories, dark, painful memories, rampaged through her brain. Her body felt as if it were reliving the whole tragedy again. Her heart rate jittered into a stupid over-compensatory tachycardia, and she squeezed the door handle.

It was all too much.

In her scrubs pocket her phone vibrated and

chimed 'Charge of The Light Brigade'. She grabbed it, grateful of the reprieve. The labour ward. 'Look, seriously, I've got to run.'

'Doing what you do best.' He flicked his thumb up the corridor, his voice raised. 'Go on, Izzy. Go ahead and run. But remember this—you walked away with no explanation, you just cut me adrift. Whatever happened back then wasn't just about you. And while I've thought about it over the years it's hardly kept me awake at night, until Isla hinted at some momentous mystery that she's sworn not to talk about, and if it involves me then I deserve to know why.'

Isabel glanced at the phone display, then up the corridor, where she saw a few heads popping out from rooms, then darting back in again.

She looked back at Sean. She thought about the dads in the delivery suites, so proud, so emotional, so raw. How they wept when holding their newborns. She thought about Tony, who'd have fought tooth and nail for his son, even if it had riled every member of hospital staff. She thought about the babies born sleeping and the need for both parents to know so much, to be involved. They cared. They loved. They broke. They grieved. Both of them, not just the mums.

So damn right Sean deserved to know. She'd hidden this information for so long, and yet he had every right to know what had happened. And once he knew then surely he'd leave? If not because it was so desperately sad, but because she had kept this from him. He'd hate her.

But the relief would be final. She'd be free from the guilt of not telling him. Just never, *never* of the hurt.

She opened her mouth to say the words, but her courage failed. 'Please, just forget it. Put it behind you. Forget I ever existed. Forget it all.'

'Really? When I see you every day? Forget this?' He stepped closer, pinning her against the doorway, and for a moment she thought— hoped—he was going to kiss her again. His mouth was so close, his scent overpowering her. And the old feelings, the want, the desire came tumbling back. They had never had problems with the attraction; it had been all-consuming, feral, intense even then. It was the truth that she'd struggled with. Laying bare how she felt, because she was a Delamere girl after all, and she wasn't allowed to show her emotions. Ever. She had standards, expectations to fulfil. And dating Sean Anderson hadn't been one of them. Certainly carrying his child never was.

His breath whispered over the nape of her neck. Hot. Hungry. Sending shivers of need spiralling down her back. He was so close. Too close. Not close enbugh. 'What's the matter, Izzy? Having trouble forgetting that I exist?'

And what was the use in wanting him now? One whiff of the truth and he'd be gone.

But, it was time to tell him anyway.

'Okay. Okay.' She shoved him back, gave herself some air. She made sure she had full eye contact with him, looked into those ocean-blue eyes. She was struggling with her own emotions, trying to keep her voice steady and level, but failing; she could hear it rise. 'We had to finish, Sean. I didn't know what to do. I was sixteen and frightened and I panicked. I had to cut you out of my life once and for all. A clean break for my own sanity if not for anything else.' She took a deep breath. 'I was pregnant.'

He staggered back a step. Two. 'What?'

'Yes, Sean. With your baby.'

CHAPTER TWO

'WHAT?' THIS WASN'T what he'd expected at all. Truthfully, he'd thought she'd been embarrassed about being seen with him. A lad from the wrong side of the Delamere social circle with two very ordinary and dull parents of no use to the Delamere clan. Or perhaps a bit of angsty teenage intrigue. Or possibly some pubertal mental health issues. But this…?

He was a…father?

Sean's first instinct was to walk and keep on walking. But he fixed his feet to the floor, because he had to hear this. All of it. 'Pregnant? My baby? So where is it? What happened?' Two possibilities ran through his head: one, he had a child somewhere that he had never seen. And for that he could never forgive her.

Or two, she'd had an abortion without talking

it through with him. *His child*. Neither option was palatable.

She followed him back in to the OR and looked up at him, her startling dark green eyes glittering with tears that she righteously blinked away. With her long blonde hair pulled back into a tight ponytail she looked younger than her thirty-three years. Not the sweet delicate creature she'd been at school, but she was so much more, somehow. More beautiful. More real. Just…more. That came with confidence, he supposed, a successful career, Daddy's backing, everyone doing Miss Delamere's bidding her whole life.

But her cheeks seemed to hollow out as she spoke. 'I lost it. The baby.'

'Oh, God. I'm sorry.' He was an obstetrician, for God's sake, he knew it happened. But to her? To him? His gut twisted into a tight knot; so not everything had gone Isabel's way after all.

She gave a slight nod of her head. Sadness rolled off her. 'I had a miscarriage at eighteen weeks—'

'Eighteen weeks? You were pregnant for over four months and didn't tell me? Why the hell not?'

So this was why she'd become so withdrawn over those last few weeks together, refusing intimacy, finding excuses, being unavailable. This was why she'd eventually cut him off with no explanation.

She started to pace around the room, Susan's notes still tight in her fist. 'I didn't know I was pregnant, not for sure. Oh, of course I suspected I was, I just hadn't done a test—I was too scared even to pee on a stick and see my life change irrevocably in front of my eyes. I was sixteen. I didn't want to face reality. I…well, I suppose I'd hoped that the problem would go away. I thought, hoped, that my missing periods were just irregular cycles, or due to stress, exams, trying to live up to Daddy's expectations. Being continually on show. Having to snatch moments with you. So I didn't want to believe—couldn't believe…a baby? I was too young to deal with that. We both were.'

He made sure to stand stock-still, his eyes following her round the room. 'You didn't think to mention it? We thought you'd be safe—God knows…the naivety. You were pregnant for eighteen weeks? I don't understand…I thought we talked about everything.' Clearly he'd been mistaken. Back then he'd thought she was the love of his life. He'd held a candle up to her for the next five years. No woman had come close to the rose-tinted memory he'd had of how things had been between them. Clearly he'd been wrong. Very wrong. 'You should have talked to me. Maybe I could have helped. I could have…I don't know…maybe I could have saved it.' Even as he said the words he knew he couldn't have done a thing. Eighteen weeks was far too young, too fragile, too under-developed, even now, all these years later and with all the new technology, eighteen weeks was still too little.

The light in her eyes had dimmed. It had been hard on her, he thought. A burden, living with the memory. 'I spent many years thinking the same thing, berating myself for maybe doing something wrong. I pored over books, looked at research, but no one could have saved him, Sean. He was too premature. You, of all people, know how it is. We see it. In our jobs.'

'He?' His gut lurched. 'I had a son?'

She finally stopped pacing, wrapped her arms around her thin frame, like a hug. Like a barrier. But her gaze clashed with his. 'Yes. A son. He was beautiful, Sean. Perfect. So tiny. Isla said—'

'So Isla was there?' Her sister was allowed to be there, but he wasn't?

'Yes. It all happened so fast. I was in my bathroom at my parents' house and suddenly there was so much blood, and I must have screamed. Then Isla was there, she delivered him...' Her head shook at the memory. 'God love her, at twelve years of age she delivered my child onto our bathroom floor, got help and made sure I was okay. No wonder she ended up being a midwife—it's what she was born to do.'

He wasn't sure he wanted any more details. He had enough to get his head around, but he couldn't help asking the questions. 'So who else helped you? There must have been someone else? An adult? Surely?'

'Evie, our housekeeper.'

'The one who turned me away when I came round that time? Not your parents?' He could see from Isabel's closed-off reaction that she hadn't involved them, just as she hadn't involved him. He didn't know whether that made him feel any better or just…just lost. Cut off from her life. After everything he'd believed, he really hadn't known her at all. 'They still don't know? Even now?'

'No. Evie took me to a hospital across town and they sorted me out. Because I was sixteen the doctors didn't have to tell my parents. I never did. They were away at the time, they wouldn't have understood. It would have distressed them. The scandal—'

'Of course. We always have to be careful about what our Melbourne royalty think.' He didn't care a jot about them now and he hadn't back then. They'd cosseted their daughters and he'd struggled to get much time alone with her despite his best efforts; over-protective, she'd called them. Of course, he knew better now. But even so, Isabel had been nothing more than a pawn in their celebrity status paraded at every available opportunity, the golden girl. The darling Delamere daughter who couldn't do any wrong.

No...that wasn't what he'd believed at the time, only the intervening years had made him rethink his young and foolish impression of her. When they were together he'd come to love a deep, sensitive girl, not a materialistic, shallow Delamere. But then she'd cut him off and he'd been gutted to find out she was the same as her parents after all. But this news...and to keep it to herself all that time. Who the hell was she? 'And that's why you broke off our relationship? That's why you sent my ring back to me? No explanation.'

She fiddled with her left ring finger as if that ring were still there. 'I didn't know what else to do, to be honest, I was stressed out, grieving. I'd lost my baby. It felt like a punishment, you see. I hadn't wanted him, but then, when I lost him I wanted him so badly. And seeing you, telling you, would have brought back all that pain. I wasn't strong enough to relive it again.' She'd walked towards him, her hand now on his arm. 'I'm sorry, Sean. I should have told you.'

'Yes, you should have.' He shook his arm free from her touch. He couldn't bear to feel her, to smell her intoxicating scent. To see those beautiful, sad eyes. And to know that she'd let him live all those years without telling him the truth.

He forced himself to look at her. To imagine what must have been going through her head at that time. The fear, the pain, the confusion. The grief. It must have been so terrifying for a young girl. But still he couldn't fathom why all of that had been a reason to shut herself off from him. To keep all this from him.

She looked right back at him, not a young girl any longer. She was a beautiful, successful woman with tears swimming in her eyes—tears that did not fall. She wiped them away. It was the first time he'd seen any emotion from her in the months that he'd been here. Now, and when she'd kissed him back in Melbourne. There had been a few emotions skittering across her face back then: fear mainly, and a raw need. 'Please, Sean. Please say something.'

He didn't know what to say. How to feel. Right now, he was just angry. Empty. No...just angry.

It was as if a huge chunk of his past had been a lie. He should have known about this. He should have been allowed to know this. 'I've spent all these years wondering what turned you from being such a happy, loving girlfriend to a cold and distant one literally overnight. I thought it was something I'd done and I went over and over everything until I was lost. Or that you'd had a nervous breakdown. Or that I wasn't good enough for you. I tried to see you but had the door closed in my face so many times I gave up. You refused to answer my calls. I tried hard to understand what was happening. In the end I just presumed your parents had somehow found out and banned you from seeing me.'

'They wouldn't have done that.'

'Wouldn't they? You weren't exactly thrilled at the prospect of telling them we were an item. *Let's keep it a secret,* you said. *Our secret love.* It seems you had a lot of secrets back then, Isabel.'

She flinched, so she must have remembered saying words he'd believed at the time were heartfelt. 'I didn't want to cause you any pain.

There wasn't anything you could do. I thought it would be for the best, for both of us. Just put it all behind us.'

'I could have grieved, Isabel, I could have helped you with that.' He held her gaze. 'So was it? For the best?'

She shook her head. 'No. Not for me, anyway.'

'And not for me, either. I'm sorry, Isabel. I'm sorry you had to go through that, I know how hard it must have been. But…' And it was a hell of a big *but*…what was he supposed to do now? Why hadn't she told him? Even though she'd lost their baby, did that mean she'd had to throw their love aside too? He couldn't think straight. Just looking at her brought back hurt, and more, stacked alongside the fact that he'd been a dad. He'd had a son. And he hadn't even known.

Words failed him. 'I can't imagine your state of mind, you're right. But one thing is for sure. If I'd known something like that that deeply involved someone else, someone I'd professed to care about—to love, even—I'd have mentioned it.'

She hung her head. 'It was a long time ago. We have to move on, Sean.'

'Easy for you to say, Isabel.' He was loud now, he knew his anger was spilling into his voice, his face, but he didn't much care. 'You've had many years to get over this. It's in your past. But this, this is my present right now. So you'll excuse me if I take a little time to come to terms with it all. I had a son? Wow. It would have been nice to know that.'

'Oh, yes? Well, it was horrible. I was distraught, traumatised. I was a young girl, for God's sake.' Her voice was shaky now, like her hands. 'You know what makes it all so much worse? *You.* Seeing you brings it all back, and I don't want to think about it any more. It hurts. Okay? It hurts, so I wish you'd never found me.'

You have no idea what she's been through, Isla had said when she'd encouraged him to come all this way to confront Isabel. *Don't hurt her.* No? He didn't want to do that. He didn't want to make her relive that pain.

But he didn't want to be with her either. Right

now he didn't even want to breathe the same air as her. Not after this.

A difficult silence wrapped around them like the foggy December day outside.

Her hand covered his. 'I didn't mean to hurt you, Sean. I'm sorry for leaving you to wonder all those years.'

'Yeah. Well, so you should be. Keep out of my way, Isabel. I mean it. Keep out of my way.' And without so much as looking at her again he stalked out of the room.

'You've had a major operation and a big shock to your body. Three units of blood. That's an awful lot to get over.' Isabel gave Susan Patterson what she hoped was a reassuring smile. Twenty-four hours post-op many patients felt as if they'd been hit by a truck. But because they always, always put their babies first they tried to recover far too quickly. 'The good news is, you're making an excellent recovery. Your blood pressure is stable and your blood results are fine. We're going to move you from High Dependency back to the ward so you can be in with the other mums, and we'll bring baby up to be with you. He's ready to leave SCBU now. Between you both you've kept us on our toes, but things are definitely on the way up. He's a little fighter, that one.'

'He's got a good set of lungs, I'll give him that.' Susan gave a weak smile back. Kicking back the covers, she tried to climb out of bed. But when her feet hit the floor she grabbed onto the bed table for stability. She was still a little pale, and Isabel made a note to keep an eye on that. It wasn't just haemoglobin she needed to watch, it was Susan's desire to do too much too soon.

'Hey, there's no hurry. Rest easy. I'll ask a nurse to come help you have a shower. That scar's in a tricky place, so you need to support it when you move. And remember, Caesareans do take longer to recover from, so don't expect too much from yourself.' Glancing at the chart, she realised Susan's baby was still listed as Baby Patterson. 'Have you thought of a name for that gorgeous wee boy yet?'

Doing as she was told, Susan sat down on the side of the bed; a little more colour crept into her cheeks. 'We had thought about something Christmassy like Joseph or Noel, but as he was early we had to change all that. If he'd been a girl I'd have called him Isabel.' Her cheeks pinked more. 'After you, because you did such a great job of saving us both. But instead we thought we'd choose Isaac. It has the *Is* in it—and that'll remind us of you. I guess you get that all the time?'

Isabel felt her smile blossom from the inside. 'Actually, not very often at all. It's very nice of you. Thank you. I'm honoured.'

'Oh, and Sean as a middle name. After Dr Anderson.'

Sean. Of course. Why not? She forced the smile to stay in place. 'Oh. Lovely. I'm sure he'll be thrilled.'

And she'd got through ten whole minutes without thinking about him, just to be reminded all over again.

Last night had been filled with internal recriminations that had intensified in direct proportion to her wine consumption. From: she should have told him years ago, to...she was glad she'd kept that pain from him, to...how dared he be so angry? She'd been the one going through the miscarriage. She could choose who she disclosed that information to.

But the way he'd looked at her had hurt the most. He'd shut down. Shut her out. The light and the vibrancy that she'd always seen in him had been extinguished. He hadn't even been able to look at her. And that had been her fault.

And now...now that she thought about it, she realised that he had a very disturbing effect on her. Even after all the intervening years she still found just looking at him made her mouth water, made her heart ache for more. Thinking about that kiss made her...

'Isabel? Dr Delamere?'

'Oh, sorry. I was miles away.' Now she couldn't even focus on her job properly. First and last time she'd let that happen. It was Maggie, one of the ward clerks. 'I have a message from Jacob. He wants to see you in his office, as soon as you can.'

'Oh, fine, thank you.' Isabel turned to excuse herself from her patient. 'I'm sorry, Susan, but

Jacob's the boss around here, so I'd better get going. I'm off to Paris tomorrow for a conference with him. But I'm so glad we managed to get you on the road to recovery before I go.'

'Paris? Lucky you.' The new mum looked almost wistful.

'No. You have a husband and a lovely family. I'd say you are the luckier woman right now.' Isabel tried to put all thoughts of Sean out of her mind. Once upon a faraway innocent time she'd dreamt of having what Susan had: a husband and family. But the thought of risking her heart again left her more than cold. Terrified, in fact. She just knew she couldn't survive that kind of loss again.

So seven days away from Sean would be the perfect antidote. She could lose herself in the bright lights and the Christmas markets and the lovely amazingness that she'd heard Paris was—oh, yes, and she had work to do, at least, for the first few days. 'I'll pop in this evening, Susan, to make sure you're okay before I head off. In the meantime, be good and rest up.'

Thinking about which boots to take with her to

Paris…and deciding, oh, what the hell, she'd take all three pairs…she sauntered along the corridor to Jacob Layton's office. She was just about to tap under the Head Obstetrician sign on his door when she heard voices. Two men. Not happy.

What should she do? Knock and enter? Wait?

Ah, whatever, she'd been summoned, so she knocked.

'Isabel.' Jacob opened the door with a frown. He seemed flustered. Not his more recent relaxed self, but more a throwback to the days when he used to have the nurses quaking in their boots. Maybe things hadn't been going so smoothly with him and Bonnie. But they seemed fine, beyond happy even. Or…worst-case scenario, maybe he was sick again? The man had a habit of keeping too much to himself and not allowing others to share the load.

'Hi, Jacob.' Instinctively she put her hand out to his arm. 'Are you okay?'

'Yes. Fine.' He stepped back from her hand, looking a little alarmed. No, embarrassed.

'Are you sure? You look—'

'I'm absolutely fine. In all respects.' Not one to

expand on anything personal, he gestured her to come into the office. 'But I need to talk to you… both.' He nodded towards Sean, who was standing at the far side of the office, looking out of the window, hands thrust into his trouser pockets. Everything about Sean's manner screamed irritation. Anger.

He turned. 'Isabel.'

'Sean.' So they were down to monosyllables. Okay, she could live with that for the next five minutes. But, dang it, her heart had another idea altogether and tripped along merrily at the sight of him standing here in a dark-collared shirt and asset-enhancing charcoal trousers, all grumpy and angry and so very, very gorgeous. Why did he have to look so damned delicious?

He always looked delicious to her, she realised, with a sudden pang in her tummy. Even when he was angry. But that wasn't important, couldn't be important.

'Look. You're not going to like what I'm going to say. So…' Jacob beckoned them both to sit down '…I'm just going to cut to the chase, here.'

'Why? What's the problem?' Something inside

Isabel's gut tumbled and tumbled. She looked from Jacob to Sean and back again.

Sean shrugged. 'We are. Apparently.'

Jacob shook his head. 'I'm sorry to say, I need to talk to you about an incident yesterday. An argument, between the two of you.'

Blood rushed to her cheeks. Isabel couldn't believe it. She'd never had so much as a frown about her behaviour, never mind being involved in an 'incident', as if she'd been rude or unprofessional or worse. It had been a private conversation, opening her very shattered heart. 'Someone complained about it? A patient?'

'No, not a patient.' Her boss looked a little red-faced. 'This meeting is unofficial and won't go down on your records, unless...well, let's just say, if you can resolve this situation amicably...'

'What situation?' Uh-huh. Of course. Sean hadn't been happy about what she'd told him yesterday, he felt betrayed and now he wanted to get his own back by getting her fired? Surely that was too underhanded even for him? That would be callous and bullying and very unlike the Sean she'd known. But she didn't know him now, really, did she? They'd been apart too long. He wouldn't…would he? She turned to look at him. 'Did you make a complaint, Sean?'

His blue eyes fired black. 'Don't be ridiculous. Of course not.'

Jacob's hands rose in a calming gesture. 'No, no, it wasn't Sean. It wasn't a complaint. *I* overheard a lot of arguing yesterday in the OR. Raised voices. Personal things were said. It made for unpleasant listening—which, I might add, was unavoidable and a few other people overheard too. The staff now think they're going to have to work in world war three, dodging bullets flying between you two.' Jacob leaned towards Isabel. 'I know I've been difficult, I know I can be a grouch, but I hope I never had cause to raise my voice or make everyone feel as if they couldn't work with me.'

He'd been sick, poor man, and had wanted to keep that to himself. He'd told no one and borne the weight of the department's needs along with his illness. He deserved a bloody medal. And yes, he'd been grumpy too, but things had changed—in his love life, mainly—and he was a lot happier now. And well again. The atmosphere in the department had become much more relaxed, until...

'So are you saying that people don't want to work with me? That it will be awkward?' Because of Sean? This was ridiculous. Never, ever, had her private life interfered with her work. Never. She was a professional. Her work was her life and she would not let anything get in the way of that. Damn Sean Anderson. Damn him for making her life hell all over again.

'No,' Jacob continued. 'I'm saying that I can't have my top obstetricians in such discord. You need to be able to assist each other, to work together at times. I want a harmonious atmosphere when I come to work. Not Armageddon. My staff deserve that, the patients certainly deserve that and so do you if you're going to do the job well.'

Sean nodded, and his reaction was surprising. 'Things got a little heated, I admit. It won't happen again.' She'd expected him to level the blame at her, but instead he wore it. He continued, 'We will be back to situation normal as soon as we leave this room. You have my word on it.' But Sean didn't look at her and she knew from the tightness in his shoulders and the taut way he held his body that he was livid, and only just about managing to keep it together in front of the boss.

And he was right, of course. They had to be normal and civil with each other, for the sake of their colleagues and their jobs. Their patients deserved the utmost professional conduct, not two senior doctors fighting over something that happened years ago.

But still...she didn't know if she could face him and be normal. Not after the way he'd looked at her. And definitely not after the kiss that still haunted her.

She needed time away from him, that was the answer. Although, she ignored the nagging voice in her head that told her that seventeen years apart from him hadn't made a huge difference to her attraction to him. This time she'd make it work. She'd erase him from her life. She'd go to Paris and teach herself all things Zen and meditate or something, she'd learn the huffy aloofness of Parisian women, she'd become sophisticated…and she'd come back immune to his generally annoying attractiveness.

'Yes, you're both right. Things got out of hand and it won't happen again. You and I are off to Paris tomorrow, Jacob, so we can all put this episode behind us. When I get back things will very definitely be back to normal.' She felt better already.

Jacob scraped his chair back and stood, signalling the conversation was coming to an end and that he now wanted them to act on their word. 'Actually, Isabel, I need to talk to you about Paris. Unfortunately, something's come up and I can't go. I'm going to have to leave you to do the presentation on your own. I'm sorry.'

'Oh. Okay.' Not so bad. Paris on her own would be wonderful. Perhaps she could play hooky a little and do some sightseeing? Have a makeover?

Her boss scrutinised her reaction. 'You'll be fine, don't worry.'

'I'm not worried at all. It'll be great. But I thought you wanted to schmooze the SCBU ventilator manufacturers for some discounted prices?'

'I'm sure you can manage that just fine.' He started to walk them both to the door. 'And Sean will be on hand to help.'

Isabel screeched to a halt. 'What? Sean? What?'

Sean looked as incredulous as she did. 'What the hell...? Absolutely not. No way.'

Jacob shook his head to silence them. 'I need two representatives over there to handle the schmoozing requirements and networking meetings. You're both rostered on over Christmas when we're short-staffed, and currently we're a little top heavy—no one tends to take leave just before Christmas, it's a vacation dead zone. So, it makes sense to send you together. I'll have the documentation transferred into your name by the end of today, Sean, and a synopsis of who you need to speak with and when. Who knows? A little *entente cordiale* might do you both some good.' Like hell it would. 'Really, I don't care. I just need two reps there and a harmonious atmosphere here. Got it?'

'No.' Isabel's mouth worked before her brain got into gear.

'No?' Jacob stared at her.

'I mean, yes.' No. She couldn't go with Sean. Four nights in Paris with her ex-lover who could heat her up with one look and freeze her bones with another. She needed space from him, not to be banished to a damned conference hotel with him. 'This is—'

Ridiculous. Painful. Harmful.

So, so stupid.

But if they couldn't sort it out amicably it would go down on their employment records—and who knew what else, a warning? No way. She wasn't going to let this ruin her, so yes, they needed to sort it out once and for all. But that meant she was going to be stuck with him in the famous city of love with harsh memories and increasing desires and a whole lot of tension, trying to sort out a situation that was far from normal.

'That is, if you don't kill each other first. Now, I'm running late for another meeting, so if you'll excuse me.' Jacob's word was final. 'Play nicely, children. I'll see you when you get back.'

CHAPTER THREE

'WHO THE HELL has a symposium just before Christmas?' Sean lugged his duffle bag onto the train, threw it onto the overhead rack and sat down opposite Isabel.

Angry as he was with the whole situation, he couldn't help but note that she looked as pulled together as any self-respecting Delamere girl would be. A dark fur-trimmed hat sat on her head, her straight golden hair flowing over her shoulders. A smattering of mascara made her green eyes look huge and innocent, and her cheeks had pinked up from the bitter north-easterly that had whipped around them as they stood on the Eurostar platform. A red coat covered her from neck to knee. At her throat was a chain of what looked like diamonds. They weren't fake. He knew her well enough to be sure of that. She looked like an Eastern European princess rather than a doctor.

And, despite himself and the rage still swirling round his gut, he felt a pull to wrap her in his arms and warm her up. *Damn it.*

She barely took her eyes away from the glossy magazine she was reading. 'It was originally planned for September, but had to be postponed because of a norovirus outbreak at the hotel the day before it was due to start. That's smack in the middle of conference season so all the other appropriately sized venues were already full. This was the only time they could rebook it. So we're stuck with it.' Now she lifted her head and glared at him. 'Like I'm stuck with you. But I won't let that spoil my time in Paris.'

She was angry with him? 'Whoa. Wait a minute. Let's backtrack a little…you're pissed with me because of what exactly? Because I don't remember me keeping any secrets from you for the last seventeen years.' The train was beginning to fill. People were taking seats further down the carriage, squealing about Christmas shopping, so yes, he knew this wasn't the time or the place.

But she answered him anyway, her voice quiet but firm. 'Sean, I apologised for that and I cannot do anything about it. You want to keep going over and over it, feel free but it won't change a thing.'

Her eyes clashed with his in a haughty, assertive glare. She was not going to move on this, he could see. But he could see more than that too. He could see how tired she was. How much she was hurting. How the proud stance was a show. And he felt like a jerk. She'd been through a traumatic time and had achieved so much despite it.

And how she had him feeling bad about this whole scenario he couldn't fathom.

Dragging a book from his backpack, he settled down. It would get easier, he asserted to himself, being with her. He'd get over the swing of emotions from anger to lust. He'd get bored of looking at her. Surely? He would stop being entranced by that gentle neckline, the dip at her throat where the diamonds graced the collarbone. He'd get tired of the scent...expensive perfume, he guessed, but it was intoxicating nonetheless, sort of exotic and flowers and something else. *Her...*

Now, where was he...? Ah, yes...neonatal emergencies...distraction therapy.

As the train jerked to depart she closed her magazine and gazed out of the window. Luckily the seats beside them were free; they had the four-berth area to themselves. 'I've never been to Paris before.'

For a minute he thought she was talking to herself, then he realised it was actually an attempt at a civil conversation. Fine, they were in a public place. He could do civil just to get through the two-and-a-half-hour journey. But that would be as far as it went. 'It's a great place. I went a few years ago, when I did my gap year. I travelled around Europe for a bit.'

An eyebrow rose. 'I didn't know you did a gap year?'

'There are lots of things you don't know about me, Isabel. There are years and years of my life you know nothing about, and you've spent the last couple of months that I've been here running in the opposite direction whenever I'm around too. Hardly surprising you know nothing at all.'

'I know.' Tugging off her coat and hat, she plumped up her hair and looked at him. 'I'm sorry. After what I told you yesterday you'll understand that I just couldn't deal with you being back in my life again.'

Guilt could do that to you, he mused. 'And now?'

She shrugged a delicate shoulder. 'Now I don't have a choice. Thanks to Jacob.'

'Indeed. So let's make a deal, shall we?'

'Depends what it is?'

'We'll attend this conference as a team to represent the department. But after that, in our downtime, you don't get in my way and I won't get in yours.' That should do it. No cosy dinners, no shared intimacies. He could revisit some old haunts, discover new ones. On his own. He stuck out a hand.

'Fine by me.' She took it, her eyes widening at the shot of something that zipped between them as their palms touched. Heat burnt her cheeks as, with equal force, it seared through him, wild and unbidden, shocking in its intensity. For a moment she locked eyes again with him; this time he saw fire there. Then she let go and wiped her palm down her trousers as if trying to erase any trace of him from her skin. 'So, what are you going to do? In Paris? Do you have plans?'

'Oh, we're doing polite chit-chat? The ever-so-charming Delamere dialogue?'

All heat extinguished in a second, her glare intensified. 'Gosh, you really do hate me and my family, don't you?'

'Isla's sweet.' He let the insult by omission sit with her for a moment. What was that line between love and hate? He knew he was straddling something of equal measure. He wanted her, and he didn't want her. Too much either way, it was disturbing. 'I was actually referring to the way you smooth over any difficult social encounter. How easy it is for you to glide seamlessly from one meaningless subject to the next.'

'Then you don't know me at all either, Sean. You think you do, but whatever misapprehensions you have about me, they're wrong. I'm not like my mum and dad. I never was. I used to hate being paraded in front of the cameras and the elite with a begging bowl for whichever charity they favoured that month. Don't get me wrong, I loved the causes they were fighting for, but I always felt awkward and embarrassed to be there.'

He kept his face passive. 'I thought I knew you. I always believed you were polar opposites to your parents.' And even though he'd consoled himself over the years that she had just resorted to Delamere type and turned her back on him, here she was challenging him. Because he'd seen her in action, the compassion and the dedication. Truth was, he didn't know her at all now, not really. He knew what she'd once been, but the young, bright Isabel Delamere didn't exist any more—he was learning that very quickly.

And the other unpalatable truth was that he was intrigued by her. He'd found out her secret and should have packed his bags—job done, history exposed—and put her and Cambridge behind him. But now he was in forced proximity with her and, well…she was a whole new fully realised version of the girl he'd known—a more professional, more intense, more dedicated version. It wouldn't hurt to learn just a little bit more. For old times' sake. 'I guess the Delamere name would have helped your job prospects no end, though.'

They were interrupted briefly by a waiter bringing the Chablis and cheese platter Sean had ordered on boarding.

Even though they were at loggerheads she still accepted a glass of wine from him. Took a sip. Then answered, 'Just like you I got where I am by sheer hard work. My name didn't open any doors for me. Once out of the State of Victoria no one's heard of Daddy—well, a few have but no one cares. He's a neurosurgeon too, which isn't very helpful to someone who wants a job in obstetrics.'

'It can't have hindered you, though.'

She shook her head. 'Whatever you want to believe, you clearly have it all worked out. But in reality I'm just bloody good at my job. I certainly don't have to prove myself to you; my competence is between me, and my patients. Who, I might say, have ranged from a pre-eclampsic mum in Kiwirrkurra, to a too-posh-to-push minor British royal and everything in between. So get off your high horse, Anderson, and give me a break.'

'You worked in Kiwirrkurra? I didn't know that. Impressive.' Kiwirrkurra had to be one of the most remote areas in the country so up-to-date technology and equipment would have been lacking, not to mention the barren, dry heat that shrouded the place. Not many would have been able to cope with the workload and unpredictability of outback medicine. It was the desert, for God's sake; somehow he just couldn't imagine Isabel there. 'How the hell did you keep your diamonds free from all that red dust? Must have been a nightmare.'

'Well, I didn't take—' She paused…looked at him…shook her head again, eyes rolling. 'You're pulling my chain. Ha-bloody-ha. Well, let me tell you, it was *so-o-o* hard, the dust got everywhere, and I mean, everywhere. I had to polish my diamonds every night before I went to bed.'

'Yeah?'

'Nah.' But there was a smile there. It glittered,

lit up her face. And for the first time since he'd been in this hemisphere it felt as if there was a breakthrough between them. Tiny, compared to what they'd had years ago—or at least what he'd thought they'd had—but it was something they could hang the next week on instead of all this anger-fuelled bile. She laughed then. 'Well, you still know how to wind me up, I'll give you that.'

'Too easy, mate. Too easy.'

She had some more wine. 'Tell me about your gap year.'

How to capture the wealth of experiences in one conversation? 'It wasn't much different from a lot of people's to be honest. I took the year off between university and internship. Went to India to do some volunteer work at a community hospital—went for a month, stayed ten. Then took two months to see some of Europe.'

Her eyebrows rose. 'Must have been interesting, India?'

He laughed. 'Interesting is definitely one way to describe it. It was hard, harrowing, enlightening and liberating too. Maternal death rates are diabolical. Infant mortality's the same...all for the sake of a little bit of knowledge and some simple resources. Running water would be a good start.'

'You always were altruistically minded. You wanted to save the world. You wanted to achieve so much. And clearly you have. Do you remember when we—?'

'Anyway, when I was in Paris…' He cut her off, not wanting to do any of that Memory Lane stuff. He didn't want to remember that all-consuming passion they'd shared—for life, for their futures, for each other. The soft way she'd curled around him, the kisses. She might have let her guard down a little but he needed to make sure that his was firmly in place.

She'd already shattered his heart once—offered no explanation at the time and expected him to accept the new status quo, her rules: no questions asked. What were the chances she'd changed? Very little. And maybe she was right, maybe he didn't know her now, but he knew she was all but married to her job. He knew she could be single-minded when she wanted. And, if her actions at sixteen were anything to go by, she didn't allow anyone into that private part of herself. Not really.

So yes, while he could be convivial and keep the peace and put up a decent social front, he was better to be always on guard when it came to Isabel Delamere.

'Best thing about these conferences is the extra-curriculars, right?' Phil, the man sitting on her left, a portly GP from Hastings, nudged Isabel's side with a conspiratorial wink and clinked his glass against hers. All around the long wooden table people swirled and sipped and laughed and chatted in a dozen different languages trying to identify flavours that Isabel was sure shouldn't be in wine. *Petrol? Asparagus?*

'Yes. Well, I guess so. This is particularly fun. Any excuse for drink.' Although, she'd probably had quite enough on the train. Any more and she might lose her good-sense filter. Thankfully they'd had check-in at the hotel and registration for the conference before coming out on this delegates' do, so she hoped the lunchtime wine had cleared her system. The only downside to the trip so far—apart from Sean's presence—had been finding out that his room was next door to hers, so any downtime activities he'd be having in the City of Love had better not take place in their hotel. She did not want to hear that through the walls.

'Ah…' The man next to her laughed. 'I detect a funny accent. Aussie, are you? Or Kiwi? I can never tell the difference.'

She gave her new friend a smile. 'No one ever can outside of the southern hemisphere, apparently, but we are very proud of our differences. And our wines. I'm Australian.'

'It's a bit like the league of nations here—that guy over there, Manuel, he's from Spain and Natalie's from Belgium.'

'Nice to meet you.' It was lovely to be surrounded by such a diverse group of people. Phil seemed pleasant enough, but even though Sean thought she was the queen of small talk Isabel just didn't feel in the mood tonight, which kind of went against the whole conference spirit. Thank goodness Phil wasn't one of the people she needed to schmooze, because schmoozing was the furthest thing from tonight's wish list.

Before she got embroiled in any more conversation she looked down the table to the woman standing at the end leading the wine-tasting, and noticed things were getting started again. 'Oh, she's talking. All this swilling and sniffing...I'm never going to get the hang of this.' Isabel listened intently and tried to think about the taste of biscuits and did Madame really say pomegranate? Isabel wasn't sure she could taste anything other than, well...wine. But she wasn't going to admit that.

It was lovely. It was. The wine was delicious, pomegranate or not. The atmosphere in the ancient stone wine cellar—*le cave*—was cosy and lighthearted. She was in Paris! She'd had a glimpse of the Eiffel Tower, and the amazing old buildings and the Seine River and it all looked breathtakingly beautiful, like a film set. She should have felt on top of the world to be here. Drinking wine. Lots and lots of different kinds of wine, with clever, articulate people. But something was niggling her.

And he was sitting to her right.

All six feet one inch of dark and distracting niggle.

By some cruel twist of fate the organisers had placed him next to her. Which did not adhere to the *keep out of my way* game plan. The seating had been arranged so they were all squashed in along narrow benches that meant that she couldn't forget him. She could feel him. Couldn't keep out of his angry gaze. Couldn't ignore him chatting up the beautiful French midwife on his right.

Brunette. Stacked. Young. Hanging, open-mouthed, on his every word. The dashing, antipodean doctor with stories of daring deliveries in deepest Rajasthan. Damn him. It was hard not to listen, as Isabel, too, was mesmerised by a history she knew nothing of.

'"*Rabies!*" my colleague was shouting. "This camel has rabies, get me off, I want a different one!"' Sean was entertaining their half of the table now. His smile engaging, his drawl lilting and captivating. 'He was half sliding, half scrambling round this poor animal's neck in his hurry to get off it. I told him not to be such an idiot. It wasn't rabies—male camels foam at the mouth to attract mates. "He's not sick," I said. "He just fancies you, mate." You should have seen his face...'

I could have been there, Isabel thought to herself. They'd planned volunteer work abroad. They'd planned a future. And instead of listening to his adventures she would have been the one retelling them. Oh, damn...this wine was going to her head and making her maudlin.

Paris, she reminded herself. *I am a Parisian woman. I care not for ze ex.*

The very beautiful Frenchwoman at his side seemed to have forgotten her haughty Gallic woman-warrior roots and was flicking her long bouncy curls in a very flirty way as she tilted her head back and laughed at Sean's story.

'Very good. Very funny.' Isabel patted Sean's arm and gave the brunette a hard stare before flicking her own hair and snagging her fingers in it. 'Ouch. I...mean... Can you please pass the crackers?'

Flicking and flirting were way out of her comfort zone. She made a mental note to practise in the comfort of her hotel bedroom.

'Of course.' Sean turned around and gave her a weird look as she dragged her fingers through a knot and grimaced, before he flashed her a lovely wide smile. And she was the only one in the room who knew it didn't have an ounce of authenticity to it. 'What do you think of the wine, Isabel? As good as back home?'

'Oh, I don't know...' She looked at her surroundings, breathing in the age-old aroma of fermenting grapes and oak barrels, and sighed. 'There's something about Paris... Sacrilege, I know, but everything seems better here.'

'Even me?' This time his grin was real. And her gut tightened in response. He was joking with her, and she was aware that she'd drunk more than her fair share of wine, so yes...he did seem a teensy bit better. Not that she was about to admit to that.

The newly adopted Frenchwoman in her wanted to throw him a disdainful shrug as if he were but crumbs on ze floor, but the Aussie in her came out fighting. 'Ah, Seany Boy, I don't want to burst your bubble, but there's only so much that grog goggles can enhance.' And so that had been a little over-loud and rather more matey than she intended.

His voice again, close to her ear. Too close. Was it hot in here? 'Are you okay, Isabel? It's been a long day. You look a bit flushed. You sound a little…tense.'

Hardly surprising under the circumstances. 'I'm fine, thank you for asking.' The wine-tasting woman was handing out small glasses of something that looked like cough syrup. That made how many glasses they'd each consumed? Isabel didn't dare to think. 'Too much of this, I guess. I'd better be careful.'

'Spoilsport. We're in France—you need to chill a little.' He swirled the stem of his glass before he looked at her again. 'Vivienne and a few of the others are thinking of going to a club after this…'

'Vivienne?'

His confused frown deepened as he flicked his thumb to the woman on his right. 'Yes, Vivienne. She's from Aix-en-Provence.'

'Lucky her. She's very pretty.'

He shrugged. 'Yes, she is.'

A pang of something Isabel didn't want to acknowledge, but knew damned well was jealousy, arrowed through her tummy. He wasn't hers to pine after. She'd made sure of that years ago, and to hammer that message home she'd spilled her secret to him and watched any kind of hope shrivel. 'Well, have fun. At the club. With Vivienne.'

He grinned, eyes darting to the long dark tresses, the flicking. 'I intend to.'

I bet you do. Irritation rising from her stomach in a tight, hard ball of acid, Isabel tried to wriggle her feet out from under the table, which was easier said than done. 'Really? You can't wait until I've gone?'

'What the hell...' he growled, his voice hard and low, '...has it got to do with you?'

'Because...' *It hurts. Because*—she realised with a sharp sting in her chest—*I want you to look at me like that, as if you're anticipating a delicious treat.*

Definitely too much wine.

The best idea would be to leave him to it. Really, the best idea would have been not to allow him to come in the first place. No, the best idea… She sighed. Why was it that the best ideas always happened after the event? She finally managed to get her feet out from the bench and tried to stand up, wobbling a little, then losing her balance in her new high-heeled suede boots. 'Oops.'

Quick as a flash he caught her by the arm and steadied her. 'Are you okay?'

'Oh, for goodness' sake, I just wobbled. I'm fine.' But she wasn't, not now. At the touch of his hand on her bare skin, desire fired through her. It had been so long since she'd felt it, so alien to her, it was a shock. All at once her body craved more touching. More touching him. More everything.

Oh, God. She looked at his broad chest covered in a crisp white collared shirt. At the model-worthy jawline. At that smiling mouth that seemed to mock and tease and was still so damned kissable. At those dark eyes boring into her. But most of all she felt his heat against hers. And she realised, with even more disbelief, that she wanted Sean Anderson in her bed.

Which was…well, it was surprising. Ever since she'd lost the baby her sexual experience had been marred by a deep-seated fear of getting pregnant; she'd been uptight and never really enjoyed herself. And she'd always felt, strangely, as if she was betraying Sean. So she hadn't really explored that side of herself.

Of all the idiotic things. Of all the pointless wanting… She could not want him. After all, he'd made it very clear that he didn't want her at all. And who could blame him?

But it was happening. And not only that, his breath was whispering across her neck sending more and more shivers across her body. 'Do you need a hand getting home, Izzy?'

She edged away from the heat. 'Not at all. I'm a big girl now. Besides, don't you have *la belle* Vivienne from Aix-en-Provence to consider? I don't want to cramp your style.'

He blew out an irritated breath. 'Really?'

'Yes. Really.' She could hear her voice rising and struggled to keep it low and steady so the others couldn't hear, particularly the hair-flicking lady. 'I'm just saying what I see. It's clear as day that you have plans for later. And we all love extra-curriculars, right?'

Sean's hand dropped from Isabel's arm and she could sense the rage rippling through him. His eyes darkened beyond black. His voice was hushed but angry. 'You made it very clear a long time ago that there was nothing you wanted from me. What the hell do you expect me to do? Keep hanging on? Because I will not do that, Isabel, I have my own life to live. I won't wait around for you to decide what you want.'

'I'm not asking you to.'

'Funny, because that's not how it seems to me. You don't want me to go with Vivienne? You don't want me to have fun, that's for sure.'

'Never in your wildest dreams, Sean Anderson, would I ever want anything from you. It's too late for that, way too late.'

'And whose fault is that?'

As if she didn't know already.

His words were like daggers in her heart. And he was so close, too close. His mouth in kissing distance—which was such an inappropriate thought right now, but there it was. Her heart thumped in a traitorous dance.

'Whatever. Go, do what you like. I'm leaving now anyway.' Biting back her anger as much as she could, Isabel looked from Sean to Vivienne to the rest of the table, who were grinning in the candlelight and had no idea of the shared history and the huge amount of balls it was taking just to be here with him at all.

She needed to get away from him. To put their past life far behind her. To put this new attraction back where it couldn't hurt her. Who'd have thought it, but after seventeen years of fighting she needed to get over Sean Anderson all over again. And fast.

CHAPTER FOUR

TWENTY MINUTES AND a decent dose of fresh cold Parisian air later, Isabel was feeling much more in control. The walk—or rather, the angry stamp—back to the hotel allowed a good view of the Eiffel Tower down the Champs de Mars, and oh, what a spectacular light show as it changed colours; red and green like a Christmas tree, then the tricolour and then so many different colours it was enchanting…or it probably was to anyone else, but everything was tainted with their stupid argument and the feelings of jealousy and hopelessness raging through her.

Added to the glorious sight of the Eiffel Tower there were strings and strings of twinkling Christmas lights draped along the street lampposts and trees, giving the whole place a really magical atmosphere. She'd never been anywhere cold at Christmas so this year was going to be a first. It was already breathtaking—or might have been if she hadn't been struggling for a calming breath anyway. If she wasn't mistaken there was a hint of snow, too, in the cool breeze that whipped around her cheeks and blasted Sean from her skin.

Just about.

She decided not to think about him any more. She was in France to enjoy herself, so that was what she would do.

Except…she couldn't get him out of her head. Annoying man! Annoying hormones that made her want him and want to run from him at the same time.

The claw-foot bathtub in her en-suite was just about overflowing with lavender-scented bubbles, a small nightcap of red wine was sitting on the window ledge, and if she craned her neck to the left she could see the street Christmas lights from the bathroom window.

A quick bath. A peruse of her presentation, then bed. If she could sleep at all with her emotions still coating everything she did. She slipped the white fluffy bathrobe off and stepped one foot into the warm water, stiffening quickly at the sharp rap on her door.

Probably housekeeping. Or room service— not that she'd asked for anything. But who else would it have been at this time of night?

Sean?

And there was a mind meld of thought process. Unlikely—Sean was out with a beautiful woman.

Another knock.

Ignoring the mysterious tachycardia and excitement roaring through her, she told herself not to be so stupid; it was probably someone knocking on the wrong door. She wrapped the bathrobe around herself again, and pattered one dry, one wet foot to the door. Through the little eyeglass she could see a man. *Sean.*

No. Not when she'd managed to flush him to the darkest corner of her brain. Not when she was pretty much naked. Not when she'd realised that these lurching feelings about him were a heady combination of guilt and lust. Which had to be the worst kind of concoction of hormones, surely? Especially when the lust was not reciprocated and the guilt just made him glare at her with anger in his eyes. What did he want now? To gloat? What to do?

Pretend she was asleep? Yes. Good idea. She turned her back to the door and held her breath. He would go away. She would sleep. She would be fine tomorrow.

'Izzy?' The knocking recommenced. 'Isabel, for God's sake, woman, open the door.'

Starting to feel a bit light-headed from holding her breath, she very slowly let the air from her lungs and said nothing.

'Isabel… You are the worst liar in the world.'

'What?' Man, he really did know how to wind her up. Irritation now skittering down her spine, she threw open the door. 'What the hell are you talking about?'

'You. You were pretending not to be here.'

'I was not. And please be quiet, you'll wake the neighbours.'

'I am the neighbours.' Shaking his head, he gave her a sort of smirk that made her heart patter and her breath hitch. 'You were standing at the door, you saw who it was and you pretended not to be here. Don't deny it. I saw the shadows changing under the door frame.'

Busted. 'So, why are you here? Seeing as you hate the air I breathe.'

'You know why. You don't get to talk to me like that. To make me think...' He scuffed a hand through his hair and shook his head. Exasperated.

'What?'

'That there's unfinished business here.'

She swallowed through a dry throat. 'What do you mean? Unfinished business?'

'For God's sake, Isabel, you know exactly what I mean. We have to deal with this.'

She shook her head. She was so confused, her head muddled with the unending ache and so many conflicting thoughts. 'I remember that we agreed to stay out of each other's way. I remember you were going to go and have fun. Why aren't you out at a club? Vivienne seemed very interested in going, and particularly with you, if all that hair flicking was anything to go by.'

'I don't care about Vivienne.' Without seeming to give any thought to how this looked, or what she thought about it, he stepped into the room, his presence filling the space. *God,* he looked amazing, all wrapped up in a scarf and heavy coat, his cheeks flushed with cold and his hair peaky. Eyes glittering with emotions, ones that she couldn't quite read but she was pretty sure were rage. And desire. Oh, yes, she could see that. Maybe he was still thinking about Vivienne?

'She'll be very upset.'

'I doubt that very much.' He looked at her, his impassioned gaze running from her hair—all shoved up into a messy clip on top of her head—to her throat, then to her white bathrobe, and lower.

Heat prickled all over her like a rash. How could a man make her feel so…so turned on with just a look? He reached for the top of her robe and ran his fingertips across the fabric, touching, ever so minutely, her skin. Pulled the robe tighter across her body.

Standing here, almost naked but for one very precarious item of clothing, she felt set alight. Swallowing was hard. Speaking, finding words,

3

even harder. He was so close and all she could smell was him and the lavender and Paris. He was so close she could have…might have… kissed him, invited him into her bath. To her bed. Her heart. Then she remembered.

Stepping away she snarled, because it was the only thing she could manage, 'You're drunk.'

'Don't be ridiculous.' And, truth be told, he looked about as sober as she'd ever seen him. He pulled the robe tighter across her chest, covering up her exposed skin. 'Do you think I'd only come here if I was drunk?'

'I can't see any reason why you'd come here at all. You hate me, Sean, you've made that very clear.'

He frowned, stalked to the console, poured a glass of red wine and sank half of it in one gulp. 'I don't hate you, Isabel. I just hate what happened—there's a big difference.'

'You said you couldn't bear to look at me.' She hauled in a breath, two; every moment she spent with him had her fired up one way or another. 'As far as you're concerned I lied to you, betrayed you, and that is unforgivable, no matter what I went through.'

He slammed the glass down. 'You think betrayal is excusable?'

'Yes, given the circumstances.'

'The circumstances were that I loved you, Isabel. You meant everything to me. And you said the same to me, over and over. *We* created that baby.' His jaw set. 'I guess that counted for nothing? You just cast me aside.'

She felt his dismissal keenly in her chest, ricocheting over her heart, remorseless. She'd known he loved her; that knowledge had carried her for a long time. It had allowed her to excuse what she'd done in the name of protection, of love. It had allowed her to function. To grieve, and to heal. 'Your love was everything to me and, God knows, I loved you too, Sean. More than you could imagine.'

'So, that's why you kept the truth from me? Why you refused to even speak to me?'

'Yes, actually it was.' She stepped closer to him, her hand on his chest. Because she wanted to touch him one last time, because she knew there was no coming back from this. How could there be? There was too much looming between them. Too much past, too much hurt. Too much for them ever to surmount. Too much lost love. 'What was the point in ruining two lives?'

'Knowing what you were going through, what we'd lost, wouldn't have ruined my life—don't you get it? It could have made us stronger. You just didn't give us a chance. You didn't give me a chance. You shut down, hibernated your life, ran away from any contact.'

'I was protecting myself.'

'That was my job,' he growled. The rest of the wine went down his throat. 'For the first time in your life you did exactly what your parents taught you to do, Isabel, you put on a mask and pretended all the pain had gone, that you were just fine. And by doing that you closed yourself off from anyone who might help you.' He moved away from her hand as if it were a dagger, a threat. 'What a waste. What a bloody shame.'

'Yes. Yes, it is. Because you're right, what we had was special and I regret not letting you in, more than anything. Happy now?'

'You think hearing that makes me happy?'

She waved towards the door, trying not to show how much his rejection hurt on the back of so much need. She just ached to feel his arms around her, to taste him again, to make everything right between them. And it would never happen. Not now. 'There isn't any more to say. Go. Please. Just leave me alone.'

'Fine.' He stalked to the door. As he pressed down the handle he rested his forehead against the wood, took a minute to regulate his breathing. Then he turned dark eyes on her. He held her gaze for longer than anyone had ever looked at her. She saw flashes of gold in there, anger. Pain. Desire. A struggle with all three. 'What did you mean, earlier, when you asked me to wait until you'd left before I went to the club?'

Her heart hammered against her breastbone in a panicked beat. 'Nothing. I didn't mean anything by it. I'd had too much wine.' But he knew exactly what she'd meant. That she still had feelings for him. That she wanted to be the woman he took home tonight, not Vivienne.

'And now?'

'Now what?' Dangerous. Heat skittered through her abdomen. Lower.

He stepped closer and grabbed her wrist, pulling her to him, his eyes wild now, his breath quick, his growing hardness apparent. Despite everything, he wanted her.

Her ragged breathing stalled. All the tension and emotion bundled into her fists and she grabbed his coat lapels, her mouth inches from his.

For God's sake, leave.

It made no sense to Sean that he wanted to hate Isabel Delamere, but couldn't. She peered up at him with questions in her eyes. And he didn't know the answers. Couldn't tell her any more than that he was crazy with the seesawing of his head, the push-pull of attraction.

As she reached for his coat her robe fell open a little and he looked away, not willing to glimpse something so intimate. He did not want to be intimate with her; he knew what price that came with. And it was way too high for him—long, long years of getting over her. But too late, he'd caught sight of creamy skin, a tight nipple bud. And a riot of fresh male hormones arrowed to his groin.

He needed to get out.

That was about as far as his thoughts went as he lowered his mouth. She gasped once she realised what he was offering. Then her lips were on his and his brain shut down.

The kiss was slow at first, testing. A guttural mewl as his tongue pressed against her closed mouth. But when she opened to him the groan was very definitely his. The push of her tongue against his caused a rush of blood and heat away from his brain and very fast headed south. She tasted divine. She tasted of wine and sophistication. Of anger and heat. She did not taste like he remembered, a sixteen-year-old girl fresh from school. She was different, hot, hungry, and very definitely all grown woman. And he wanted to feast on her.

'Oh, God, Isabel...' Dragging his mouth from hers, he kissed a trail down to the nape of her neck, his fingers grazed the edge of the robe and he slid his hand onto the bare skin of her waist and drew her closer. She softened against him with a moan and everything finally made sense. This was what he needed. *She* was what he needed. The chaos swirling in his chest cemented into a stark hunger as he slid fingers over silken skin.

She pulled back with a smile. 'Wait a minute…I'm here wearing relatively nothing, and you're dressed for an igloo. Too. Many. Clothes.' She unwound his scarf and threw it to the floor, pushed his coat from his shoulders and let it fall. Her hands stalled at his shoulders; she stroked the thick fabric of his shirt, down his arms to his hands, which she clasped into hers. 'I can't believe…after all this time…is it what you want? Am I, what you want?'

'Do you even need to ask?' He pulled her back to him, felt her melt against his body as he plundered her sweet mouth. The smell of her drove him wild, but the taste of her pushed him close to a place he'd never been before. God, yes, he wanted her, wanted to be inside her, to hear her moan his name, to feel her around him.

She wound her hands around his neck and

pulled him closer, grinding her hips against his. He had no doubt that she wanted him as much as he wanted her, and that stoked even more heat in his belly.

Unable to resist any longer, he dragged the bathrobe from her shoulders and lay her down on the bed as she fumbled with his shirt, dragging it over his head. He kicked off shoes and socks, dragged down his jeans and then they were naked. Like all those years ago. But this was not the same. She was not the same. And he had so much more experience now—no clumsy fumblings, no teenage angst. He knew how to please a woman and he intended to please Isabel.

Taking a moment, he gazed at her face, at the kiss-swollen lips, and misted eyes. At the soft, sexy smile that spurred him on, that made him weak-kneed. Then he looked lower, wanting to feast his gaze on a body that he hadn't seen in seventeen years. And to learn about her. To re-learn what she liked. To acquaint himself with the new dips and curves, with the smooth, silky feel of her skin. The perfect breasts, a tight belly that belied a miscarriage, that a baby had been inside her.

His baby.

At once he was filled with profound and gut-wrenching emotion—she'd been through too much on her own. He should have been there with her. He should have done something. He should have known—somewhere deep within himself he should have intuitively known that she was suffering, that a part of him was inside her and broken. That she'd carried that guilt around with her for all these years, too afraid to speak of it, too scarred to share it. Until he'd pushed her…that secret was theirs, only theirs.

The emotion had a name—he didn't want to think about it.

Pushing a curl of hair behind her ear, he gave her a gentle kiss on her mouth. 'Izzy, we can't do this.'

CHAPTER FIVE

'You're freaking kidding me, right?' Isabel drew away from the best kiss of her entire life and took a deep breath. 'What do you mean? You just said you wanted to…'

'I do want to. I just don't think we should. It's late. We're probably drunk. We have to work tomorrow. And there's too much baggage and history that sits right here.' He pointed to the space between them. 'Getting in the way.'

Instead of feeling frustrated, she felt a rush of affection. God love him, he was trying to do right by her. And okay, well, she had to admit there was a teeny hint of frustration there. Wriggling closer to him, she smiled, relishing the touch of hot bare skin against hers. 'Oops, that baggage and history just got squashed under my gargantuan ar—'

'Whoa, Izzy.' His eyes lit up, the darkness

she'd seen momentarily before now gone, replaced with humour and heat. 'I've never seen you like this before.'

'I've never felt like this before.' It was true. Suddenly so hot, so alive and fired up, Isabel stroked down his naked chest. Abs that she'd never seen before, honed to perfection. Arms so muscled and strong that she felt featherlight and ethereal in his embrace. A sun-kissed chest she wanted to shelter against, to kiss, to lick… She'd never wanted a man so much in her whole life. Truth was, she'd never stopped wanting him.

He was right. What a waste of all those years. Of running and hiding and trying to cover up real deep-down feelings. Of being so, so frightened of falling in love and risking her heart all over again. 'Don't stop. We *can* do this. We can do what we want. Don't wrap me up in cotton wool, Sean. Don't treat me any differently to any of your other—'

'There are no others.'

'Liar.' She knew he was attractive to every damned woman he gave five minutes' attention to and knew, too, through the MMU grapevine, that he had a history of breaking hearts. Couldn't commit. Never gave a reason why.

'No. Not any more.' He frowned but his hand stroked the underside of her breast, sending shivers of desire rippling through her. How could she have lived her whole life never having him again? How could she have survived? Being in his gaze felt as if she'd come home to a warm cocoon after being out in a freezing wilderness. Sure, there were things to work out. A lot of things. But right now, in this room at this moment, it felt so right to be with him.

'And Vivienne?'

'For goodness' sake. She is nothing to me.'

'In that case...' she pressed a kiss onto his creased forehead '...forget the past.'

Then, she pressed a finger to his mouth to prevent him from speaking as she kissed each of his eyelids. 'You don't know me. Not really. You don't know who I am, what I want, what I need.' Her finger ran along the top of his lip; she laughed as he tried to nip it with his teeth. 'Or what I like, Sean.'

'Izzy...' There was a warning in his voice.

'This. Is. New. Everything starts from now.'
A kiss onto the tip of his nose. 'Hi, my name is
Isabel. *Isabel*, not Izzy. I am an obstetrician and
I live in Cambridge, England. I'm here in Paris
at a conference and I want to have some extra-
curricular fun.'

Then she licked across his lips, hungry, greedy
for his mouth. 'I'm very, very pleased to meet
you.' Her hand stroked down his stomach towards a very-pleased-to-see-her erection. She
touched the tip and enjoyed the sound his throat
made as he growled her name in warning.

'Isabel, you want to watch what you do with
that. It's got a mind of its own.'

'How very convenient.' She bent and licked the
tip, then took him full into her mouth ignoring
his protestations, and pushing him back against
the duvet. She could feel he was holding back a
thrust so she sucked down his length again and
again, his throaty groans spurring her on. She
loved the taste of him, the hard length. She loved
that she could make him feel so good.

'Izzy.' His hand grasped her hair and she
stopped. 'Isabel. You'd better stop.'

As she paused he shifted position, edging away from her grasp and sucking a nipple into his mouth. Heat shimmied through her. She arched her back, greedy for more, for his mouth on her body, on every part. Hot and wet. His fingers now on her thigh, higher, deeper, sinking into her core. And she was kissing him again, exploring this new taste that was laced with an old memory. His smell that was different yet familiar. His touch…my God, his touch was expert now. He knew just how to take her to the edge and tease. His erection was dangerously, enticingly close, nudging against her opening.

'You still like this?' He pressed a fingertip into her rib and she screamed.

'Stop that! No tickling. Kiss me.' She didn't want to relive anything; she wanted to create new experiences, to build fresh memories. She didn't want to look backwards. She wanted… she wanted him inside her. For a second she was serious, the most serious she'd been in a long time. Made sure she looked deep into his eyes and told him the truth. There had been too many lies between them. 'I want you, Sean. I want you so much.'

'Back at ya, kiddo.' This new kiss was slow and hard, Sean taking his time as he stoked a fire that had smouldered over the last year, burst into roaring flames over the last week and was now burning out of control. She moved against him, feeling the pressure of him, hot and hard, against her thigh.

'Condom?' he groaned, his forehead against hers. Eyes gazing down at her, startling in their honesty.

'Yes.' She held his gaze. The last time they'd done this had ended in such heartbreak. Was it so stupid to be doing it again? To risk everything once more?

He touched her cheek as if he could read her thoughts, his smile genuine, so loving and tender it almost cracked her heart. When had he become so thoughtful? So sexy and so within reach? When had he become so expert at knowing what a woman needed? When had he changed? Her throat filled because she knew the answer: in those wilderness years, without her.

His voice was soft yet filled with affection that went deeper than sex. 'It's okay, Isabel, it won't happen again. I won't let it happen again.'

Neither would she. 'Of course.' And if a baby did happen again she would tell him, she wouldn't hide anything from him. This time she'd be honest. 'In my...in my bag.'

'In my wallet.' He reached down, took out a foil, and slipped on the condom. Then he was pushing into her, slow and gentle, and she felt him fill her. So perfect. So complete. She wrapped her legs around his backside to feel him deeper. Harder.

'Oh, my God, Isabel. You are so perfect. So beautiful.' He began slow thrusts, his fists holding her wrists above her head, snatching greedy, playful bites at her nipples and her breasts. She felt captured, captivated, possessed by him. This man. This wondrous man whom she had broken as much as she was broken. And yet he put her back together again with this act.

The moves changed and the air charged. He stopped the playfulness as he kissed her hot and hard and wet. Sensation after sensation pulsed through her. She was hanging on by a thin thread. His body tensed; she could feel pressure rising as she met him thrust for thrust, joining the rhythm as he picked up pace.

His eyes didn't leave hers. His hands didn't release hers. And as they both shuddered to climax—releasing the tension coiled so deep between them for so long—she wished, *God* how she wished, she had never let him go.

'Well, wow.' Sean shifted to Isabel's side and stroked her cheek. It was the first time he'd seen her looking so bone-deep relaxed. 'I wasn't expecting that.'

'Me neither.' She shuffled into the crook of his arm, blonde hair splayed out over the pillow. 'That was very lovely, thank you.'

'Your manners are impeccable. Daddy would be proud. You sound very English all of a sudden.' He pretended to look under the duvet. 'Where's my Aussie girl gone?'

'I'm still here.' She stroked fingertips gently down his chest, her voice a whisper. 'I'm here.'

'So you are.' Something he'd never believed

possible had been possible. He tipped her chin and kissed her again. She returned the kiss eagerly. It had been amazing and surprising that intensity went so deep. A dream. Something he'd imagined for years. Making love into the night, no reason to leave. Hours and hours stretched ahead of them. Days, years. A lifetime. He'd never had the chance to do this before. Time together had been so limited, snatched moments that had ended in disaster.

He felt frustration begin to roll through him. But tried to push it back.

He wondered when he'd be able to stop thinking about the baby. The lie. He wondered if he'd ever be able to truly move on now that he knew, and he realised that moving on was something Isabel had been trying to do when she'd moved to Cambridge. It wasn't to get away from him; it was to restart her life.

So lying in bed with him probably wasn't what she'd had planned. Or him, either. In fact, this whole sex thing had pushed them across a line now and made things even less clear than they were before. And even though he'd lain awake

in many other women's beds over the years trying to work out just how to leave, he'd never felt
so conflicted about his next step.

Everything he'd said was true. She was perfect. She was beautiful. She was so much more
than he'd imagined. And he'd wanted her so
badly, for so long. All those years of wondering, of dating other women, of trying to put her
behind him. But it had been pointless because
the attraction was still there. The need. The vis-
ceral tug towards her—even though there was
danger with every step.

He wanted to think there could be a future, but
he couldn't get past the fact that she'd treated his
heart with so little respect before—would she do
the same again? Did he even want to give her
the chance? Had it, in the end, just been sex for
old times' sake?

Like he was even going to ask that dumb question. He didn't want to contemplate what her answer might be.

'What are you thinking?' Her voice brought
him back to the now.

'That you, missy, have a very important presentation in a few hours and you need to get rested up before it.' He started to pull the sheet back ready to make his leave. They both needed time to get their heads around this whole new complication. Well, he did, that was for sure. What did he actually want now? Other than a rerun of ten minutes ago.

But before he could stand up her fingers slowly tiptoed across his thigh. She spoke, her words punctuated by soft kisses down his chest. 'For some reason…I'm just not…sleepy.' Her fingers connected with his now growing erection. Because he was, after all, just a red-blooded man with the most beautiful woman in the entire universe lying naked next to him. Oh, and a whole host of emotions swimming across his chest. Yeah, his body still wanted her, regardless of the past. It was his head that was causing trouble.

Her voice was a warm breeze over his skin, tender yet filled with a promise. 'Don't know about you, Seany Boy, but exercise always makes me sleep so much better. And short of going downstairs to the hotel gym, I can only think of one kind of exercise we could do at this time of night. You?'

'Isabel—' He turned, then, with gargantuan effort, to tell her. To put some distance between his feelings and his needs. But the trill of her mobile phone jolted her upright.

'Oh. Who could that be at this time?' Wrapping a sheet round her, she grabbed her bag from the floor next to the bed and pulled out her phone. 'It's Isla. What would she—? Oh? The baby? D'you think?' Throwing Sean an apologetic look, she pointed to the phone. 'I'm so sorry…but I've just got to get this. I won't be long.'

And so he was surplus to requirement. It was a decent enough excuse to regroup and rethink. To get the hell out, and work out what to do next.

Isabel watched the door close behind Sean and blew out a deep breath. Getting her head around whatever the hell had just happened would have to be banked until after she'd spoken to Isla. But she got the feeling he hadn't been able to get away quickly enough. Maybe he was having second thoughts, too? 'Isla? Isla, are you okay?'

'Isabel. Oh, my God, Isabel.' The line was crackly but she could still hear her sister's voice filled with wonder. 'He's beautiful. Perfect. I can't believe. Oh…'

'You've had the baby?' Isabel's heart swelled and she fought back tears. Her sister was a mother. She hadn't been there for her. Her mouth crumpled as she forced words out. 'Oh, sweetie. How was it? Are you okay? Is he okay? A name? What happened—aren't you early? Was Alessi there?'

Clearly having a better handle on things than Isabel, her sister drew a sharp intake of breath and began, 'Okay, I can't remember which question was first. You have a nephew. A gorgeous, gorgeous nephew, all fingers and toes accounted for and lots of dark hair like his daddy. Born three hours ago.'

'Oh, wow. Three hours? You were going to phone me when you went into labour.' Isabel stopped short. Three hours ago she was busy. With Sean. Speaking to her sister wouldn't have been the best thing to happen. But maybe if they had been interrupted she wouldn't now have these weird mixed emotions whirling through her chest. What they'd done had made things more complicated, not less. 'Oh, wow, I'm so happy for you. Mega congratulations, little sis.'

'It was all so quick, and I couldn't remember the time difference with my scrambled mummy brain—and the labour drugs—and your last email said you were going to Paris? So I wasn't sure—'

'Yes. I am. *Je suis ici*—in Paris.' *Having sex with my ex. And now I want to talk about it, but I can't.* Bad timing. All round. 'So, what was your labour like? Textbook? Knowing you it was probably textbook.'

'Quit schmoozing. It was okay. No, actually it hurt like hell...' There was a pause. 'Iz, are you okay with me talking to you about this? I mean...you know...because of before?'

Because of her own baby boy? Because he'd been too frail, too tiny to live, because she hadn't been able to protect him the way other mothers could. Hadn't been able to grow him to his full potential the way Isla had. An arrow of pain seared her heart. He would have been a teenager now, getting ready to fly the nest. She would have had all those memories, sleepless nights, first days at school...so many firsts; long hot summers, a house full of primary-coloured plastic and arguments over too loud music. Instead she had heartache and an extremely unwise choice of sexual partner. She couldn't even blame that on mummy brain.

She had to let it all go. She had to move on. Her baby was gone. Gone, but in her heart for ever. *Do not spoil your sister's day.* 'Of course, I'm fine, Isla. Talk away. I want to hear about everything...absolutely everything. I'm so happy for you. I'm just sorry I couldn't be there to hold your hand. I'm sending hugs, heaps and heaps of hugs.'

'Oh, you know I'd have liked you to be here, Iz. I would have, but you need to be away from here...I totally get it. I love you.'

Emotion constricted Isabel's throat; she had to force words out. 'I love you too.' Ever since Isla had waved Isabel off onto the flight to London she had been nothing but supportive of Isabel's need to get away from Melbourne, to put her life there behind her. To forget Sean. Yeah, that plan had worked really well. 'So come on, a name? What did you go with in the end?'

'Geo, after Alessi's brother, the triplet who died. I told you about him, didn't I?'

'Yes, yes. The baby who didn't make it...' Another one. *Breathe. Breathe.* 'That's a lovely gesture, Isla. Alessi must be so proud.' Isabel had chosen a name for her boy too but had never properly given it to him. She hadn't been able to think straight after she'd given birth, after they took his little body away. There'd been no burial. Nothing to remember him by. But she did have a name for him.

'Alessi? Proud?' Her sister laughed down the line and it was so good to hear her so happy. 'Oh, yes, and then some. He's acting like he's the only man who's ever fathered a child. Still, if it means he continues to treat me like a princess then I'm happy. I'm not allowed to move a single muscle without him making sure I'm okay.'

'Lucky you, enjoy it while you can. Give baby

Geo lots of kisses from his very happy auntie and email me some photos, now! Oh...who delivered you? Don't tell me it was Alessi?'

There was a kerfuffle in the background, familiar hospital noises—bleeps, voices. The sweet, soft snuffle of a contented newborn. 'No, he was too busy up the top end dealing with me, trying to keep me calm. Darcie was the attending, she was amazing. Very patient, all things considered. I think I may have been a bit rude to everyone, but at least it made them give me more pain relief. Talking of Darcie, did I tell you...? It's all hearts and roses over here. You'll never guess who she's dating. True love and everything.'

Sometimes Isabel really missed the gossip of her home town. The familiar. 'No? Who? Spill.'

'Only Lucas bloody Elliot!'

The heartthrob of the MMU. 'Mr Playboy himself? No way! I thought you said they hated the sight of each other.' But Isabel knew that there was a thin line between love and hate—that passion came in many forms and was fuelled by many different emotions.

Isla sighed. 'It's really cute to watch actually. There were fireworks all along the way—neither of them wanted to admit they were falling in love. Little Cora's thrilled too. Now she has an auntie as well as an uncle to watch her. Quite a unit, they are.'

Hearing all the news she'd missed out on made Isabel realise just how far away from them she was. Darcie had only been in Melbourne less than a year herself, having been part of the same exchange as Isabel. In fact, Darcie would be scheduled to return to Isabel's job in a few weeks, when the year's exchange was over. 'Well, that'll cause Darcie a few sleepless nights if she's fallen for Lucas, because he's firmly committed to staying in Melbourne with his brother and niece.'

'I know. He's been such a rock for them both since his sister-in-law died. There's no way he'd leave all that behind. But I hope it won't mean you're not coming home? Your job will still be open if she decides to stay here, right?'

Isabel had a brief image of her and Sean arriving off the same flight hand in hand stepping onto Aussie soil. Then she shook away such a fantasy. But whatever happened, she was definitely going home. And soon. 'Absolutely. Try and stop me. Oh, I do miss you all.'

'We miss you too. They all say hi.' It seemed the labour drugs were still in Isla's system as she chatted on oblivious to the fact it was five o'clock in the morning for her. 'Come home soon. I want you to meet Geo. Oh...and talking of babies...more goss hot off the press. Oliver and Emily are looking to adopt another baby. So sweet. Toby's growing into such a lovely boy and they want to add to their family.'

Another MMU romance—seemed there had been quite a few recently. Something in the water. Obstetrician Oliver and midwife Emily had been having marriage problems back when Isabel had been there; it was good to hear that they'd managed to put their rough past behind them. It was good to hear that at least some re-kindled relationships could work.

She'd bet that Oliver hadn't hot-footed out of the bedroom at the first opportunity. 'I'm glad things worked out for them in the end. Their marriage was put under so much pressure struggling with IVF. It was hard for them to see beyond that. Time makes such a difference.' Geez, she could have been talking about her and Sean. But there wouldn't be any happy endings for them. Not with the way he'd looked as he'd left. She couldn't help the yearning in her voice. 'But now everyone sounds so settled and happy.'

'They all want to know what you've been up to. Have you met anyone?' There was a pause, then Isla cleared her throat. 'How's Sean?'

What to say? *Hot sex is epic. It's the aftermath that's the problem. How to move on from here?* 'He's...he's okay. Actually, he's here in Paris with me.'

'What the hell? What do you mean? Here's me rabbiting on... Have you told him?' For a woman who'd recently given birth, Isla was very animated. Those pregnancy hormones were amazing. Isabel had seen some women act as if nothing earth-shattering had happened—popped out a baby and gone straight back to normal life, thank you very much. 'Are you...? You know...?'

We just did. 'It's just a conference.'

'Nothing's *just* a conference if Sean's there. You're away with him? Isabel? In Paris?' A loud squawking zinged down the phone line. Voices. A lot of loud garbled language. Greek? Cries, a loud hullabaloo. Then Isla was back. 'Sorry, hon. I've got to go. Geo's hungry, I think. Alessi's parents have just arrived. It's chaos. I'll call you. Call me. Talk soon. I love you.'

And she was gone. Isabel's head was spinning. There was never enough time to chat properly and the long-distance hum always interfered. She wanted to sit down and talk to her sister, to hold her precious nephew. She wanted to go home. A few more weeks and she would…only a few more weeks until the end of this contract. And then what?

She scrunched up the Egyptian cotton sheet in her hand and looked down at where Sean had been lying a few moments ago. Remembered how good he had made her feel. And how easily he'd slipped away. So instead of *then what*, it was, *now* what? Now how to face the elusive Dr Anderson?

Isabel had absolutely no idea.

CHAPTER SIX

ISABEL NEEDN'T HAVE WORRIED. There was no time for chatting at breakfast with Mr Incubator doing all the talking. No chance to catch up over lunch as she'd been cordially invited to the speaker's special VIP luncheon. Then after her presentation she'd been whisked away on a tour of the Sacré-Coeur followed by dinner and a show in Montmartre, which, it appeared, Sean, or rather Jacob when he'd registered, hadn't signed up for. And after all that French flavour she was good and ready for bed. To sleep on her own.

And no late-night visits. She didn't know whether to be relieved or disappointed.

Turned out there was rather more of the latter than she expected.

The next day flew by with more meetings— one a real success with the promise of a hefty discount on some new high-tech monitors— and interesting talks all round. She only had one more day to dodge Sean's questioning eyes, then he'd be heading back home and she'd have a couple of free days to shop. The French baby clothes were so gorgeous and chic, she just knew Isla would adore them; Isabel had no problem hanging on to spend time perusing and indulging her new nephew.

Right now, though, she was spruced up ready for the gala dinner and surveying the majestic ballroom for someone to hide behind. And yup, no Sean as yet. Thank goodness. She still had no idea what to say to him. But if she zipped towards the medical-rep crowd she might be able to get stuck in a conversation before he arrive—

'Wow, Isabel. You look amazing.'

Too late. His hand was on her waist as he drew in close and pecked French *un-deux-trois* kisses on her cheeks. She closed her eyes briefly at the sensation of his touch on her cheek, his aftershave mingling with his sunshine and sex scent. Goddamn, the man was irresistible.

But she was measured in her response. He

couldn't hike out of her room after sex without an explanation. She needed to know what was going on in his head.

Hers was a lost cause.

'Oh, this old thing? Just something I threw on at the last minute.' She looked down at the midnight-blue silk shift dress that had cost the best part of a week's salary but, hell, it had been too beautiful to resist with its teeny shimmery jewels round the halter neckline and the cutaway back. She eyed her favourite sparkly silver sandals, then her gaze strayed onto him and she almost lost her balance. The man was drop-dead hot in a black tuxedo.

Worse, she knew how hot he was out of it too. And so that wasn't helping her equilibrium, not at all.

'Well, you're just too damned beautiful. Drink? Because I need one if I'm going to spend all evening looking at you, not allowed to touch you.' He took her elbow and steered her towards the bar. 'And I get the feeling you're avoiding me because every time I turn around you've disappeared.'

She drew her arm away. 'Oh, trust me, I know that feeling. Wham, bam and suddenly you're gone.'

'What are you talking about?' He leaned over the bar and gave the barman his order, then turned back to Isabel, his eyes widening as the penny dropped. 'Oh. You're cross because I left you to talk to your sister in private? Really? Or are you cross because I didn't come to your room last night?'

'Shh…people will hear.' Not that there were many people in earshot, but…well, really.

'I don't care who hears. *Did* you want me to come to you last night? Should I have?'

She looked down at the mahogany bar because that was safer than looking into those dark eyes and saying one thing but thinking the opposite. Yes, she'd wanted to sleep with him again. Had lain awake for hours imagining him naked in bed, the wall between them a barrier she hadn't been able to bring herself to cross.

Because she didn't want to want him so much, and put her world into free fall again. She didn't want to hand over that part of herself that she'd kept safe for so long, the memories and emotions locked away. She didn't want to feel anything. And right now she was feeling a lot of things. Mainly hot and bothered and very turned on. But more, complicated things she didn't want. 'Mmm.' That should do it. Nonchalant and un-defined.

'Mmm? What the hell does that mean? Listen, Izzy, the truth is, I thought, seeing as we hadn't spent any time together talking, that it would be...I don't know, to use an old-fashioned word, unchivalrous to expect a booty call. But that was what you wanted? Yes? You wanted me to be unchivalrous?' His mouth tipped up, the grin widening as his hand smoothed round from her waist to the back of her neck, sending ripples of desire through her. His mouth was close to her throat. 'Go on, admit it. You wanted me.'

'No.' *Yes.* She couldn't help the smile. How had it gone from complicated to sex? From difficult to downright easy? Was it that straight-forward? To stop thinking and start doing? She made sure she looked right at him. 'No.'

'Next time, say it and mean it. You wanted a

booty call?' He nodded and smirked. 'Noted, naughty girl.' Then he handed her a glass of bubbles. French. Yummy. 'So, we're celebrating?'

'Sorry? Why?'

'Isla's baby? Boy? Girl? All's well?'

'Sorry. Yes, a boy. Called Geo, apparently... both doing fine. She's emailed me some photos and he's desperately cute.' She took out her phone and flicked through the photos, trying to stop tearing up, because Geo was so, so gorgeous and Isla looked as deliciously happy as she deserved to be. Alessi, indeed, so proud. And far from feeling jealous, Isabel just felt her heart filled with happiness for them.

Sean tilted her chin and looked at her. 'You miss them.'

She looked away because he saw the truth inside her as if he knew her too well. 'Yes. Of course. They're my family. It's my home. My place. Coming here was only ever temporary.'

He took a drink of the champagne. 'You're not enjoying it?'

'Oh, yes. The people are really friendly, I've

had some fabulous work opportunities, like this conference. Job satisfaction is high.'

He smiled. 'The sex is pretty good too.'

'Exceptional, yes.' Her cheeks bloomed hot. She was still so new to this, she didn't know the art of flirting, but Sean made it easy today. Maybe she'd misunderstood his frown the other night or the reason he'd left. Maybe he had just been giving her space. Maybe he'd forgiven her?

Forgiving was one thing, but forgetting? She imagined that would take him a whole lot longer. It would always be there between them. Wouldn't it? God, if only she could thrash this out with Isla, the only person who knew everything.

Apart from Sean now, of course.

They walked towards a table, so beautifully decorated with silver tableware on a crisp white linen cloth and a small silver and white Christmas tree centrepiece. He nodded to the other guests sitting there, pulled out an empty chair and indicated for her to sit. 'So tell me, Isabel, why did you really come to the other side of the world? All this way away from your family?'

She sat. 'To develop my skills and knowledge. To take part in an international study and hopefully open a new Australian strand of it when I go back to MMU.' That was what she'd told them over the video interview anyway. There'd been no mention of running away from her ex because his questions made her uncomfortable. Made her remember things she'd prefer to keep under lock and key.

'So you'll be going back when your exchange has finished?'

'If my job's still there—I get the feeling that Darcie might want to stay in Melbourne. Apparently she's hooked up with Lucas.'

He grinned. 'Really? Now that's something I'd never have predicted. They'll keep your job open for you too, though, surely?'

Isabel sighed. 'Yes, I hope so. That was one of the conditions of the exchange. I'm ready to go back, to be honest. I've had my year of living dangerously.'

'Not nearly dangerously enough.' His eyebrows peaked and his smile was as dirty as could be mustered at a dinner shared with two hundred delegates. 'There are a few things I have in mind that you could do. Only takes a bedroom. Well…not even that really. A willing mind.'

Her body was willing, it was her closed-off mind that she was having trouble with. To stop herself from slapping a kiss on that smirking mouth she desperately tried to keep the conversation on a civil track. 'And you? Will you stay here or move on somewhere?'

He shrugged. 'I haven't decided yet. My contract runs for a couple more months…then I'll make some decisions. I'm registered with a locum agency in London, so I may just stay in the UK for a while, perhaps see what Edinburgh's like. I'm happy moving around for now but I guess at some point that'll grow old. I like the challenge of new places, meeting new people. I like not having to commit to one place. There's a lot more to the world than Melbourne.'

Her heart began to hammer a little uncomfortably. 'You'll want to settle down at some point, surely? Family?'

And she didn't even know why she was asking him such a question…it wasn't as if that kind of life was anything she'd been working towards. She was happy being on her own, making her own decisions, living the single life. Wasn't she? At least she had been. A bit lonely, perhaps, but nothing serious.

Maybe that tiny ache in her gut that she'd tried to ignore was a reaction to Isla having a baby. Yes, that was it. Isabel decided she was a little unsettled by that, that was all.

The food arrived, and even though it might have seemed a little rude to ignore the other diners Isabel just wanted to sit and listen to Sean; his voice was lyrical and smooth. 'My parents have hinted about grandchildren. No, make that, my parents ask about potential wives and babies every time I phone or email. It's like something out of the eighteenth century. Neither of my brothers look like they're settling down either, so I'm in the firing line.'

'Your parents are lovely. How are they these days?'

'Same as ever, working hard on the business. Dad's still in accounting and Mum's still doing his paperwork, but she craves grandkids and won't leave me alone.'

Isabel laughed, remembering the not so subtle hints her father had been dropping about continuing the Delamere line. 'Mine too. So hopefully they'll be appeased by Isla's bub and leave me alone now.'

Sean looked surprised. 'You don't want that for yourself?'

And risk the chance of losing everything again? 'No.'

He paused to eat some of the amazing chicken pâté and bread, then continued with a frown, 'But you always used to talk about having kids—a whole mess of them, I think you said. You wanted to be a different parent from yours, you were looking forward to chaos.'

'You remember things I don't remember saying. And anyway, people can change, can't they?'

He put his knife down and turned kind eyes towards her. 'Not that much, Izzy. You can't give up on a dream because of one knockback. You help women achieve that dream every day—you can't tell me that things have changed so irrevocably for you?'

The food was tasteless now, a lump in her throat. 'A knockback? Is that what you call it?'

'No. That's not what I meant.' His voice grew darker. 'I could call it a lot of things. And I'm trying to deal with it…but damn it—'

'I'm sorry, Sean.'

'I know you are and so am I.' He shook his head, his fists tightening around his crystal wineglass stem. 'I promised I wouldn't hark back to it because just thinking about it makes me angry.'

He probably would never get over it—she hadn't, not really. But he had to deal with her lies as well as the loss. 'I've given you my reasons.'

'I'm trying hard not to be angry with you. I understand why you kept it from me. I'm angry about the whole sad scenario, Izzy. But you can't let it scar you for ever.'

'I've told you, I'm not Izzy, not any more.'

'And I don't know who you're trying to kid, but I'm not buying it. Older, yes. Wiser, definitely.

More confident in lots of ways…apart from intimacy, which is a shame. Because that would be cool—you deserve to have that in your life. I'm betting that inside you're still the same girl who desperately wanted a family. A husband. The things everyone wants. And I bet that it's worse now that Isla has it. You're Izzy the girl, in here where it matters.' Touching just above her heart, he seemed to resettle himself, shake the demons away, and she envied him that. Or maybe he was just better at sorting his head out? 'Don't think for one moment that I'm belittling anything. I'm not. I know what you went through. I can't imagine what it was like to have it happen so young…so alone.' His hand covered hers now and the feel of him there…just there… made everything seem so much better. 'You said yourself, it happens. You have to look forward.'

She didn't want to be that frightened girl any more; she'd worked hard to be someone else. But yes, he was right about the intimacy—she didn't know how to let herself go, not on many levels. She hadn't dared. As far as she was concerned intimacy led to heartbreak. She knew it because she'd lived it. 'As it happens, I am trying to move forward and let go…that's the real deep-down reason I came to England in the first place. I needed to get out and breathe a little. Get away from you.' She nudged him playfully. 'But then you keep turning up like a bad penny and bringing me right back to the beginning.' Creating the same wild feelings she'd had when she was a teenager. Only this time they were more intense, more enduring. More potentially painful.

'You think? A beginning?' He frowned. 'Is that what you want to do? Start again?'

She rubbed her fingers across strong, skilled hands that had brought so much life into the world. 'I have no idea. I haven't dared want anything. It's too painful to risk going through all that again.' But he almost made her feel as if she could take a chance. She looked up into eyes that seemed so understanding and she felt as if she could pour her heart out to him. But that would surely send him running to the hills. So she deflected. 'What do you want?'

She didn't know what she wanted him to answer. She just hoped it was somehow in sync with what her heart was telling her. That maybe, just maybe, she could work things out with Sean. Start afresh. If they both had enough courage. At least for a little while, they could have some fun and then she'd be gone and so would he.

He laughed. 'Hell, Isabel, it's messed up. I'll be honest with you and say I've gone round in circles. I've worked back and forth across the world, travelling thousands of miles just to get you out of my head and each time I end up back with you. I can't tell you straight up that I'm one hundred per cent okay with any of this. But I do know what I want right now, right this second. That's the best I can do.'

'Oh, yes? What do you want?' But she had a feeling she knew already. Just one look at the gleam in his eyes…

He paused as a gentleman stepped up to the stage and said something in French. The room hushed. There was applause while another man walked up to the microphone, all big smiles and wide arms as if giving the room a warm hug. She looked across to the woman opposite her and laughed when she laughed. Hopefully at some point there'd be a translation. But all Isabel was aware of was Sean next to her. The heat. And her unanswered question.

There was a break in proceedings as the microphone screeched, a brief technical hitch, and an embarrassed smile from the compère. Suddenly Sean's voice was in her ear, warm and deep. 'I want to peel that dress off you...very slowly. I want you and me naked.'

'Huh?' She swallowed, with difficulty. Her mouth was suddenly very dry. If she turned her head she'd be mouth-to-mouth with him and the temptation to kiss him was overwhelming. Where Sean was concerned there were no half measures, no light feelings; it was intense and deep and raw.

'I want to be inside you again. I want you, Isabel Delamere, with every ounce of my being. I want to kiss every inch of your stunning body.' He withdrew his hand from hers and placed it on her thigh. The heat and tingles arrowed in waves straight to her belly as he circled his fingertips towards her core. 'I don't understand what that bloke's talking about on stage. I don't understand much of the stuff that's in my head because it's like a washing machine all churned up. But I do know that I want you. Now. And I don't think that feeling's going to go anywhere for a while.'

She turned and whispered back, barely able to form words. 'It's bad, isn't it?'

Suddenly her heart began to thump in anticipation. Adrenalin surged through her veins and fired her nerves. Two people. That was what they were, just two people taking what they needed. No one was going to get hurt. She'd built that protective barrier around her heart over the last years; it was strong and sturdy; she knew what she was doing just fine. He was thinking of going travelling, she was thinking of going home. It was just two people taking what they wanted while they had the chance. They'd missed out on so much already. She dared to reach out and put her hand on his thigh too and felt the contraction of muscle at her touch. Heard his sharp intake of breath.

He growled. 'It's very, very bad. And yet somehow we keep ending up here. Maybe it's time to stop pretending and accept reality. This isn't stopping any time soon. There's nothing either of us can do.' He wrapped her hand in his and pushed it further up to his groin. Her fingers made contact with his growing erection. 'Hell, Izzy, it's bigger than both of us.'

'Good lord, it's very big indeed.' She knew he was fooling around, but she didn't want this to end. It was like a dream, a fantasy. 'Maybe when you go back to Cambridge and I stay here for a few days things will get back to normal again.'

'What exactly is normal? At each other's throats? Not speaking? Shouting? Not seeing you for too many years? Not sure I want to go back to any of that. I do, however, want to go back to bed, with you. Or, not bed…I have an idea.' He leaned in close and whispered, 'How about now? A night together. Then, what say we play hooky tomorrow? Have some fun in Paris?'

'We're supposed to be working.' Okay, so she said it out loud just for the record, but she didn't mean it. The last thing she wanted was to be sitting in a stuffy conference room when she could be playing with Sean.

'Who will know? You always were such a goody-two-shoes.'

He slid his hand up inside her dress, stepped fingers towards the inside of her thigh. Here in the middle of a gala. What the hell? Daddy would freak. 'And you always were such a tear-away.'

'No wonder your father didn't like me. Miss Delamere, this is not how you behave at dinner.'

'I was thinking the exact same thing.' He was hot and hard for her. 'Besides, I don't care what he thinks.'

'I wish you'd said that seventeen years ago.'

'Okay…I'm not apologising any more for stuff that happened a long time ago. Let's plan forward.' Her raging heart was thumping so hard she wasn't sure she could breathe properly. Or make much sense past *take me now*. But for the benefit of others on the table—if they could hear—she tried to sound normal. 'I'd really like to go on the field trip to the homeless perinatal clinic in the morning…but then? Maybe we could duck out after?'

He nodded. 'I'd like to take you on a boat

ride down the Seine—we could have lunch. Then visit the Louvre… Dinner in the ninth arrondissement, I know a place…' As her hand wrapped around him he tensed, eyes fluttering closed. 'Okay. I can't take any more. Let's duck.'

'Now?' His hand was still over hers as she stroked him.

He looked as if he was in pain, or at great pains not to show any reaction at all. 'You want to spend the next two hours listening to a man droning on about maternal care in Limoges, that's fine. But I'd like to get some hot sex. *S'il vous plaît.*'

She almost choked on her champagne. '*Mais oui.* Since you asked so nicely.'

'Okay, so stay close, no one needs to see this.' He pulled her up and held her in front of him as they sneaked out the back way, then half walked, half ran to the lift. As he hit the down arrow he turned to her. His hand was on her thigh, warm through the thin layer of silk as he dragged the old-fashioned outer metal lift door to a close. Then the inner one. It jerked, then started to descend. 'You have any preference in venue?'

'None whatsoever.' She threw her head back and laughed, feeling the rasp of his stubbled jaw on her neck. The lift smelt of old leather and Paris. Of daring and adventure. Of the exotic and sophistication. 'How about here?' So she wanted to get dirty with him in the lift. That was new.

'Great minds think alike.' He jabbed the lower-floor-car-park button then pushed her against the mirrored glass, kissing her deep and hard. She pressed against him, feeling his hardness between her thighs. His hands skimmed her body, palming her breasts, thumbs flicking gently against her nipples. Next thing, he'd untied her dress at the neck, it fell to her sides and his mouth took over from his hands, slanting over her hardened nipples.

When they hit the empty dark cavern he reached out and grabbed the metal car park sign and jammed it in between the lift doors so they wouldn't shut. The lift wasn't going anywhere. Neither were they. Pulling him towards her by his now unravelled black tie, she breathed, 'Smooth move, Dr Anderson. Very smooth indeed.'

'I like to think so.'

Then, feeling the most turned on she'd ever been in her life, she wrapped a leg round his waist. 'So, come put that clever mouth to good use.'

CHAPTER SEVEN

'THIS WASN'T QUITE what I had in mind as a date,' Sean whispered to Isabel as he handed over the steaming plate of beef bourguignon to the eighteenth homeless man of the morning. But working side by side with her gave him a punch to his gut that was filled with warmth as thick as the heated cabin they were in. After the tour of the homeless shelter and perinatal outreach clinic she'd accepted the request to help out at the soup kitchen with grace and humility. Every day she surprised him just a little bit more. Not least last night with the lift escapade. He couldn't help grin at the thought. 'Still, this stuff smells delicious, if there's any left...'

'It's for them, not us.' She kicked him gently but smiled at the dark-haired, olive-skinned young woman in front of her, wrapped in layers and layers of tatty grey cloth and a dark red headscarf. She had a full round belly and was breathing heavily. Pre-eclampsia, probably, Sean surmised—*needs assessment*. A small boy dressed in clothes more suitable for summer perched on her hip, grubby, pale and with a drippy nose. *'Pour vous, madame. Merci.'* Isabel turned. 'Actually, no, wait…oh, never mind. I want to ask about the boy, I wish I could speak the language a bit better.'

'Don't worry, the smile says it all. She understands.'

'And I want to take the tray over to the table for her, but she won't let go of it. I think she's so glad to get some food she won't take a chance on losing it.'

'Then let her manage if that's what she needs to do.' The kid looked feverish. 'He's not looking too great. When they're done I'm taking them both over to the clinic.'

Isabel let the tray go. 'It's zero degrees out there and look at the poor state of them both. It's Christmas in a week or so—what's the bet he's not going to have the best day?'

The boy coughed. Wheezed. And as he

breathed out he made a short grunting sound. He didn't smile. Or cry. Thick black rings circled sunken brown eyes. Mum didn't look much better. Pregnant. Homeless. Sean pointed to the boy and made a sad face. Mum shook her head and jabbered in a language that didn't sound French. Then she handed the child towards him.

Sean took him, noted his flaring nostrils as he struggled to breathe, and felt his forehead. 'He's burning up. He needs a good look over. I'll take him through to the clinic now.' He gesticulated to the mum to follow him, but she clearly didn't understand. He tried again. Made another dramatic sad face and pointed to the boy. Mum shook her head again and tried to grab the tray of food and her son back.

'Okay, okay.' Sean held his palms up in surrender and let her take the boy. She clearly wasn't going to let the kid out of her sight, regardless of where she was and the minimised risk. And she was determined to get that hot food in both their bellies before they went anywhere. Not such a bad idea, all things considered. But the child needed help and soon. 'Eat first.'

She squeezed into a chair at a small melamine table and in between greedy gulps tried to feed the boy some of the meaty gravy, but he slumped down and shook his head. She tried again, jabbering in a smoky voice, cajoling him. Pleading with him. And still the boy didn't open his mouth.

Eat. Sean felt an ache gnawing in his gut. *Eat, kid. For God's sake, eat something.* He watched fat tears slide down the mum's cheeks and wondered just how awful it would feel not to be able to provide for your child. To not be able to make him better. To not be able to feed him. That ache in his gut intensified. How helpless must Isabel have felt to not be able to grow her baby, to lose their son? And he hadn't been there for either of them.

Sean had never been helpless and he wasn't about to start now. He was three steps towards them before mum looked up and shook her head.

He turned to Isabel. 'His breathing's laboured. Bluish lips. Exhausted. Won't eat. He's going next door, now.'

'I'll come with you.' Obviously seeing the danger too, Isabel nodded, handed the plates over to some of the other volunteers from conference and between them they managed to get mum to follow them into the outreach clinic. As they tried to lay the boy onto a trolley he had a severe coughing fit, then went limp.

'Quick. Oxygen. Come on, kiddo. Don't give up on us.' Sean checked the boy's airway and grabbed a mask and Ambu bag, wishing, like Isabel, that he could speak the mum's language. Or even the language of the health-care workers. But luckily they all spoke the language of emergency and in a flurry of activity anticipated what he needed, drew up blood, cleared secretions, put in an IV line—eventually. The boy was so dehydrated that finding a vein was almost impossible. 'Come on, buddy. Come on, breathe for me.'

As he watched the kid's chest rise and fall Sean blew out a huff of relief.

He caught Isabel's eye as she stood waiting with an intubation tube. 'I think we're good. He's settling a little. Pulse rate down from two twenty to one sixty. But we need blood gases and a blue light to the nearest hospital. Probably a bolus of antibiotics to be on the safe side. Who knows what the French is for that?'

Dr Henry, whom Sean and Isabel had met earlier on the clinic tour, appeared from the kitchen and explained in his very decent English that the paramedics had been called. The boy would be given the best care available at the public hospital and he thanked them very much for the help.

Mum, meanwhile, was another issue. As she stood and watched them working on her son a keening cry came from deep in her throat as if he were being ripped from her body. She refused to let go of the boy's hand, getting in the way of the staff. They tried to encourage her to take a step back. She pushed forward. In her confusion and distress she became more and more distressed. In her world, control was key. One wrong foot and you lost what precious little you had.

'It's going to be okay. It's going to be okay. Come with me, love. Let's sit down, shall we?' Isabel took her hand and gently pulled her away, wrapping an arm round her dirty clothes and walking her to a quiet corner of the room. The clinic was a prefabricated building with curtains delineating cubicles—the little fella's crisis had stopped any other consultations from happening and all eyes were on the emergency. A perinatal care centre they might have been, but an emergency care facility they definitely weren't. 'They're doing good. He's sick, but he'll be okay.'

Mum clung to Isabel and jabbed a finger towards the trolley. 'Teo. Teo.'

'The boy?' Izzy smiled and pointed towards the child. Her calm demeanour seemed to have an effect on the woman as she stopped gesticulating quite so frantically. 'His name is Teo? He's beautiful. And he's going to be okay. He's with Sean, and Sean won't let anything bad happen.'

Now that belief in him was another hard punch to his gut. She believed in him? She believed in him.

'*Oui.* Teo.' This was getting surreal. The woman was speaking French now to Isabel.

Isabel nodded, smiling, and pointed to the woman's belly. 'Another baby there?'

Mum rubbed her stomach and sighed, dejectedly. *'Copil mic.'*

Taking her hand, Isabel monitored the lady's pulse. 'Hey, Sean, hand me that sphyg, will you? I'll take her blood pressure while I'm here. I have no idea where she's from. Are there any translators?'

'I'll grab Dr Henry when he's finished. Oh, wait…he's just there.' They waited until the doctor sauntered over.

Isabel took it from there. 'I'm a bit worried about her, blood pressure's skyrocketing—I think she's pre-eclampsic; swollen feet…I need a urine sample but I don't know how to ask. Kid's sick and she's scared for him—it's not helping. And I have no idea where she's from. What do you do about language barriers?'

The doctor shrugged. 'It happens all the time, we have a good network of translators. I'll call one in.' He turned to the mum. 'Romania?'

'Oui.'

'She's from Romania? Wow. That's a long way from home. Who's looking after you? Where do you live? Will she have to pay for her medical treatment? Because I don't think she'll be able to. I'm sorry, I have too many questions and none of them in French or Romanian. Pretty useless, really. I don't even know her name.'

Dr Henry gave her a big smile, because, really, who wouldn't? 'That's okay, Dr Delamere, you care, it is enough. We have about twelve thousand homeless people in Paris and many of them are immigrants. But we also have good medical facilities to look after them, if we can reach them. Many are illegal aliens and don't want to be caught, so they get lost. Or worse. She may have friends around outside—they often meet people from their home country and hang out with them. Or she may have no one. I didn't see her come in with anyone. You?'

Isabel shook her head. 'No. She was on her own, and, in this state, that's a very scary place to be.'

Sean looked over at the kid and thought about Isabel all those years ago, on her own, dealing with the worst thing possible. That would be how this mum felt right now—even worse, she didn't understand what was happening and couldn't communicate. But she'd quietened down since Isabel had befriended her, so he wasn't going anywhere. 'So we'll stay with them until we get her and the boy into a stable state.'

'Are you sure? You don't mind?' Isabel was still holding the woman's hand, which she stroked as mum gave a small sheepish smile. 'We'll stay with you. It's okay. It's okay.' Then she turned to Sean. 'Thank you. I know you had things planned.'

Nah. Other than give her the best doctor award? The boat cruise would have to wait. 'I'm not going anywhere apart from to check on Teo. I'll be right here with you.' His heart swelled just watching her compassion. So much for guarding his heart; where Isabel was concerned it seemed she was determined to blast it wide open.

Two hours later as they stepped out of the maternal and paediatric hospital onto the Rue de Sèvres, Isabel inhaled deeply and tried to stop the hurt in her heart. 'Wow, that was an eye-opener. But thank you for staying. I don't know how I'd have felt if we'd just left them all alone.

By the sounds of it Marina lost contact with her friends when she got evicted.' Thank God for Sean, too, because his quick thinking had stopped that boy deteriorating. 'I'm going to go back to the hospital tomorrow to see how they're doing.'

'You know, you don't have to. They're quite safe now. *In good hands*, as we always roll out to our patients. And they are, so cheer up.' He slipped his hand into hers, and she still didn't know how to deal with this rapid turn of events. She was holding Sean Anderson's hand, discussing patients, looking forward to spending a date…in Paris. She felt a surge in her heart that quickly evaporated. They'd done good, but she felt… She couldn't put her finger on it. He must have sensed it because suddenly he asked, 'You okay?'

'No. No, I'm not okay. I mean, I should be, I know this stuff happens. But it's still distressing to see. That poor woman, what kind of a future does she have? She lives on the streets of a city where she doesn't even know the language. She's going to be the mother of two kids under

four. She has no easy access to medical care…
Aaargh, it's so unfair.'

His warm hand squeezed hers. 'You can't
make everyone better.'

'I know. But I can help this one. I can make
one difference today and that's enough for me.
But it still makes me so cross.' Not least because there were so many little lives out there
that needed saving.

He bent and pressed his lips to hers, pulling
up her collar around her ears to protect her from
the icy wind. 'There she is. That's my girl. She's
back.'

'What do you meah?'

He ran a thumb down her cheek, making her
shudder with warm fuzzies. Didn't seem to
matter what scenario they were in, he made her
shiver with desire. No, more than that. She liked
watching him work, liked his cool calmness and
the way he put others first. Not many did that
in the precious little downtime they had. Not
many offered to spend a few hours in a soup
kitchen instead of sitting in a plush hotel eating
dainty finger food from silver platters. 'There's

the old Izzy…the spunky girl who wants to save the world. She's here. Don't tell me that you've changed, that all your dreams are different, because they're not.'

Isabel didn't want to admit anything, because right now she didn't know what she wanted— from him. From this. From anything. 'She was on her own and frightened. I've been there and I don't recommend it. One thing I promised myself back then was that if I ever saw someone else going through a hard time I'd try to help.' She looked up and down the busy street. 'Er… where are we?'

He shrugged. 'Damned if I know. I was thinking we could go to the Louvre, but I fancy some fresh air after that little adventure. You? Fancy a walk down by the river? We can grab a taxi— look, there's one.' He stuck his hand out, told the driver where to head to then bundled her inside the warm car. The journey through the Parisian streets was halted a little by congestion. Snow had started to fall and the roads became chaotic.

'Look! It's snowing. My goodness, just look.'

'Isabel Delamere, you've seen snow before.'

'I know, plenty of times. But it's just so perfect to be snowing while we're here. It makes everything seem like a fairy tale.' But then she thought about Teo and his flimsy cotton shirt and sandals and decided that whatever else she did in Paris she'd find him something decent to wear. A Christmas present. Because he wasn't exactly living any kind of fairy tale at all.

She looked out of the window and dragged a huge breath in. There was one thing she'd never confessed to anyone, one reason why she'd always hated and loved Christmas at the same time. Why she wanted to keep busy, why she'd offered to work, why she always tried to surround herself with people at this festive time and not dwell on what-might-have-beens and what-ifs.

She brushed a threatening tear away from the corner of her eye and hoped Sean hadn't noticed. She was getting too soft in her old age. Maybe it was seeing the little that Teo had and the fight in his mother. Or maybe it was being with Sean and feeling all these new emotions rattle through her that made her a little off balance.

They were let out by Notre Dame cathedral. Isabel looked up at the grand façade of the famous building. 'Amazing. I always wanted to come here. I've seen so many pictures of it, brochures in the hotel, I feel like I'm looking at something so familiar, it's almost like I've been here before. Look—' She pointed up at the huge rose window and the majestic arches. 'It's breathtaking.'

'Do you want to go inside?'

'No. Well…' There was a small part of her that wanted, for some reason, to make a special commemoration of their newfound friendship. And of the child they'd both lost. Perhaps a candle? But she didn't want to add something so solemn to the day. Didn't want to dwell on how she felt about Sean, given that things were so uncertain between them. Another day, maybe, when they were on a more even footing. She gave him a bright smile. 'No, let's walk. I want to tramp along the riverside in the snow, and, if you're not careful, hit you in the face with a snowball.'

'I'd like to see you try.'

She reached out and caught the falling snow

in her hand, watched the snow melt on contact. 'It's not snowball kind of snow.'

'Never mind—I'm sure we can find something else for you to play with.' Then he picked her up and twirled her round, pressing cold lips against hers. 'You want to go straight back to the hotel? I know a good way we can get warm…'

Oh, it was tempting. 'Yes…but I'd like to spend some time out here. It's like a wonderland. Look at that cathedral, all lit up. It's amazing.'

'In that case…' He put his hand into one of her deep coat pockets. Didn't find what he was looking for. So shoved his hand into the other one.

'What are you doing?'

'Gloves.' He pulled out her woolly gloves and shrugged them onto her hands. 'Now you're appropriately dressed, which, I might add, is a shame. I liked you a lot better with your dress round your waist.' He gave her a wink that started an ache down low in her belly and spread to a tingle across her breasts. 'But I wouldn't encourage that here—you'll get frostbite. Later… definitely.'

'Is that a promise?' Suddenly she found herself looking forward to later.

As they trudged across the square in snow that had started to stick the street lights flickered into life. Looking up, Isabel watched the swirl of the flakes as they danced around her. Sean wrapped an arm round her shoulder and she hugged into him as if it was the most natural thing in the world to do. They walked in silence for a few minutes, crossed through the souvenir stalls, round the side of the cathedral to a garden. 'If you want we can walk through the Latin Quarter…the Left Bank. We can cross over there.' Sean pointed to the left, past a large fountain and through the gardens. 'Or over there.' To the right.

'It's prettier through the gardens.' And it was; snow tickled the tree branches, coating each leaf like ice frosting.

As they walked Sean began to talk, his voice surprisingly serious. 'Isabel, is it hard for you to do your job after what you went through?'

'It's hard when I see a young frightened kid having a baby, hard when I see a difficult birth, but it's made me more resolved to help, to strive for a happier outcome.' It was actually quite a relief that they were side by side as they talked, so he couldn't see the pain she knew was in her face. Couldn't see the need for him to hold her. *And yes, it hurts like hell when things don't work.* She still shed a tear for the young mums; she felt the righteous anger when a baby didn't make it. She still felt the kind of pain that Marina had voiced earlier. Would it be different if she'd never been pregnant, never had that chance? She didn't know. 'Why do you ask?'

'I'll be honest with you—I had a different feeling in there with Teo and Marina. Watching her trying to feed him and failing gave me a gut ache like I've never had before. I felt her pain. Viscerally. I needed him to eat. I was willing the kid on. Sure, I'm driven to help them all, but this was different.'

'Empathy? You've always had empathy, Sean.'

'It was more than that. This was like a weird force in me.' He turned to her. 'You know I'd have done anything to help you, don't you? I'd have fought for that baby with everything I had.'

'I know.'

He was speaking so quietly now she had to strain to hear him. 'I wish I'd been there.'

'I know. Me too.' Her heart twisted. She tiptoed up and kissed him, hoping that whatever he felt could somehow be kissed away. She doubted it, but he pressed his lips to hers and held her close, his eyes closed, reverent. And he pulled her closer, wrapping his arms tightly around her as if she were a lifeline. An intense kiss that shook her to her soul, had her falling, tumbling into warmth. And even when there was no breath left they stood and held each other, listened to the distant traffic, to people laughing. People living their lives. People sharing, kissing, loving—taking a chance. When she eventually stepped away she felt as if a small part of her heart had been pieced back together again.

And shaken a little by the ferocity of it all.

It comforted her to have him close, but it scared her too. It was happening so quickly—they'd fallen so fast. She could lose herself in him, she thought, in *us*. She could let herself go. But what would that be like, in the end? Would it last? Or would she have to piece herself back together all over again?

That was something she couldn't contemplate. But, for now, he was here and she wanted him to know how she felt. 'I'm sorry, Sean, for the way I treated you. You're a decent, smart and sexy guy. I did bad by you, I should have been honest instead of selfishly hiding myself away.'

'You did what you had to do to cope. I understand.' They walked a little further through the tree-lined park leaving footprints in the snow, large and small behind them. Then, 'His name?'

'Sorry?' Her heart thumped.

Sean looked at her. 'I'm sorry, I have to know. What was his name? Did you ever think about giving him one?'

'Yes.'

'And did you give it to him? Did you tell him what his name was? Did he hear it?'

'Yes. I told him his name. I told him I loved him. I told him I was sorry.' *I cried it out to the skies and whispered it to the silence.* 'But then they took him away...and...I never got to hold him again.'

His lips a thin line, Sean dragged her to him. 'I'm so sorry. I'm sorry. I'm sorry.'

'It was a long time ago.' Her throat was thick with hurt, words were hard to find, even more difficult to speak. And her chest felt blown wide open.

Wrapped in his arms, she stood for a moment looking up at Sean, at his earnest face. The smooth line of strong jaw, the turmoil in his eyes. She hadn't wanted to put it there. Her gaze was drawn skywards to the fading light and the dance of snowflakes as they fluttered around them shrouding the cathedral in a magical white blanket.

The sound of bells ringing made her jump. She pulled away from him and started to walk again. As the light began to fade Isabel thought it was possibly the most beautiful place she'd ever visited. So serene through the gardens, the crisp crunch of snow the only real sound around them. Most of the tourists and hawkers had headed away, but a few stragglers remained. As they approached the stone bridge a man peeked out from behind a stall laden with postcards, mini Notre Dame cathedrals and paraphernalia.

'*Pour vous? Une serrure?* A lock? You buy?' His croaky voice made little sense.

'Keep walking. I don't know what he's talking about.' Isabel kept hold of Sean's arm as they stepped onto the bridge. The last dying rays of sun bathing the cathedral in an eerie light. 'Oh, my goodness. Look at that… What are they…? Are they locks?' Thousands and thousands of locks of all shapes and sizes covered the metal railings all along the bridge. She peered closer. 'They all have names on.'

'They're love locks, Izzy. Surely you've heard of them? People bring them here, write their names on the locks, attach them to the railings and toss the key into the Seine. Apparently if the key can't be found, the love can never be broken…or something like that.'

'"*A 4 M…*" "*Marry Me…*" "*Love You Always…*" "*Ever Mine…*" Oh, so sweet. But so many. There must be thousands.'

'And more. Look, there's another one just going on.' Sean pointed to the far end of the bridge where a bride and groom were having their wedding photographs taken, the sunset-captured cathedral in the background. The groom kissed something in his hand and then pressed it against his wife's lips and together they threw it into the gurgling water below.

'Wait here.' Sean left her side. She watched him jog back to the stallholder, who had almost finished packing up. From inside one of his bags he passed Sean something. Isabel's heart began thumping. Surely not. Surely Sean wasn't going to do something…something like… Looking over towards the bride and groom, she held her breath.

What the hell was he doing?

CHAPTER EIGHT

IF HE LET them go, Sean reasoned as he walked back to Isabel, if he pretended these keys held the past and hurled all the lies and the history and the hurt into the river, then that would be the end of it, right? He would let it all sink to the silted bottom, drowned in everyone's shared promises of everlasting love. Surely some of that would rub off onto him? Surely he'd be able to let her in? Surely he'd be able to stop thinking about it. Draw a line.

Maybe it was that easy. Maybe having her was as easy as that.

'Here.' He handed her a marker pen the guy had sold him for way more than it was worth. But how much was the price of casting off these emotions and facing her renewed? 'I want you to write our son's name on this lock.'

'What?' Her eyes widened, although there was

some relief there too—he couldn't fathom why. 'Okay, I just thought…oh, never mind.'

'Write his name.'

Her hands were trembling as she tried to take the top off the pen. He took it from her, pulled it off with his teeth and handed it back. She wrote wobbly letters across the bronze lock.

Joshua.

'I hope you like it.' She was heaving great breaths while her whole body, his beautiful brave Isabel, shook.

'Yeah. Yes, I do. It's solid. Strong. It's a good name for a fine boy.' He'd had a son, and he'd been called Joshua. Sean's chest felt as if it were being squeezed in a vice. Above and to the left of the boy's name he wrote his own, to the right he wrote Isabel.

Damn it, if his own hand wasn't shaking too. Maybe it was the freezing weather.

'He was due at Christmas, right?' He'd done the maths. They'd only had sex a couple of times so by his reckoning their baby had probably been due around December.

'Yes.' She looked away, her eyes glittering. She

gripped the top of the railings, for a moment he thought she might faint or tumble or scream, but she held her ground, staring into the distance along the river. Snow fell onto her shoulders, into her hair like tiny pearls. When she turned back her eyes were dry. 'He would have been a Christmas baby. He would have been seventeen this year. All games consoles and mobile phones. Maybe a girlfriend. Definitely smart and handsome.'

'And that's why you offered to work?'

She nodded. Her mouth about to crumple. 'Yep. I always work this time of year.'

'Oh, God, Isabel.' He pulled her close again, trying to protect her from something he couldn't stop. 'You spend every Christmas thinking about him? You must hate it.'

She let go of the railing and curled into his arms, her head shaking against his chest. 'No. Because it means I can think about him more. But…well, yes. I hate it.'

His chest constricted. She'd carried this for too long on her own. 'Okay. Let's do this.'

She nodded. Hauled in another breath; this

one was stuttered as if her lungs were blocked. 'Okay. I'm ready.'

He lifted his fist to attach the lock to the tiny speck of space they'd found amongst the other locks bearing the love of thousands of people from around the world. All that love right here in this one place, all those promises, all that up-lifting belief—he didn't know if he had it in him, but he'd damned well try.

But her hand closed over his, making him stop. 'Wait, Sean, look, there's a sign there saying the people of Paris don't want us to do this. It's damaging the bridge and the water, apparently. There's a picture of the railings collapsing under too much weight, of fish being poisoned by the toxins from the metal.'

Below them a pleasure boat chugged along, splaying dark water from either side, a com-mentary in French coming from speakers. When it had gone and the water smoothed out a little Sean peered as close as he could. There were no signs of any keys. No sign of damage. But he knew that you couldn't always see the damage. That nature had a habit of keeping that kind of thing locked deep, the harm seeping out slowly and steadily over the years, poisoning everything. Like his life. Like hers.

Not any more.

Rapidly blinking, she gave him a brave smile. 'I don't want to add to any more destruction. Can we do something else?'

He gazed down at the lock, at the names written there, and the sharp pain in his chest intensified. 'It's just a symbol, that's all.'

'Exactly. So…I suppose we should…just go.' She seemed deflated.

'Okay. I have an idea. Stay here.' He dashed back to the gap-toothed man and bought another lock—a different one with a different set of keys. Then he walked back to where she was shivering. After writing the names in the same configuration he gave her the keys to his lock. 'Take these. Now, give me the keys to your lock.'

He wrapped her fist tight around his keys. 'You have the keys to my lock—I can never open it without you. Keep them safe. These are a symbol of what we had. *Who* we had. What we lost.

All that love, Isabel. It was there, it was ours. We can't deny it or forget it, but we can honour it. And him. I want to honour him. Joshua.'

Still no tears, but her bottom lip quivered. How she held it all in was beyond him—not once had he seen her truly cry. As if it was some kind of weakness, he presumed, she wouldn't let herself break down. She took the keys and put them on a chain round her neck. 'Here. Take these keys, Sean. These are the keys to my lock. These are a symbol of what we shared. Of Joshua. Take them and keep them safe.'

'Always.' He fixed them to his key ring and put them in his inside top coat pocket.

'Next to your heart.' She pressed her palm against the pocket and he took the moment to shield her tight from the wind. From the snow that had continued to fall. From the past.

Now he had the keys to her lock, and, despite what he'd promised himself over the years, she had the keys to his heart again.

But then, the simple shocking truth was she'd always had them, hadn't she?

* * *

'Okay. No more of this. We have to get moving before we freeze our socks off.' He straightened up and gave her the first smile she'd seen from him in hours. It was gentle and honest and trusting. And with such intention Isabel watched Sean cast away the pain and the fear and the past. It was the right thing to do and yet somehow she couldn't quite let it all go. Almost all... but there was still a part of her, a tiny corner of her heart that clung to that long-ago night as if determined not to forget.

She took another huge breath and blew it out. Like cigarette smoke it plumed in the air, then was gone. The lump in her throat still lodged there though, but with every smile of Sean's it lessened just a little bit more.

'Okay.' He was right; it was time to move on. She took his hand and walked the length of the bridge, and onto the other side of the river, the lights from the old sandstone buildings reflected in the dark water. *Paris.* 'Yes. No more of this... we're in Paris for some fun and extracurriculars. Can I say, I particularly like the extracurriculars.'

His eyes glittered. 'Me too. Phil from Hastings does have a point. As did Jacob—this *entente cordiale* is good for the soul.' The hurt had gone; now all she could see as she looked at him was light and fun and teasing. His hand crept close to her bottom. 'I intend to fully indulge myself in *beaucoup d'entente cordiale.*'

'I am fully aware of your intentions, Dr Anderson. That poor lift. Those poor people waiting on the ground floor.' She grinned, remembering exactly why the lift had been halted. Dangerous. Exciting. Sex. 'So where to now, maestro?'

'The Latin Quarter,' Sean told her, filled with resolve. 'Full of quirky shops, decent cafés. There's a second-hand English bookshop along here you might like, too. Or we could stop and get your portrait done. There will be lots of opportunity between here and the Louvre.'

Never. 'My God, you're going full-out tourist.'

'I thought you might like a memento of your visit.'

She didn't need one. She had every memory

of this day engraved on her heart, and it was wide open for more. 'Not if it means staring at my ugly mug for ever more.'

At her frown he grinned. 'Okay, okay, no portrait. So it takes us about half an hour to walk to the Louvre. Of course, that depends on how many *chocolats chauds* you have between here and there. Or there's always cognac to chase away the chill. Chocolate and cognac, how's that for a combination?'

'Now you're talking.'

The afternoon was, indeed, filled with chocolate and cognac and a little red wine and a lot of kissing and many, many shops. By the time they took another taxi and did the rounds of the sparkling Christmas village at the Champs-Élysées Isabel's cheeks were pink, her legs tired and her arms filled with Christmas gifts, decorations and festive food. What a day, filled with extremes, some heart-wrenching lows and adrenalin-pumping highs. Some very, very highs.

'Okay, smile.' Sean snapped a selfie of them with nothing but dark sky and stars around them. It wasn't hard to smile; they were sitting at the top of a huge Ferris wheel—the central cog lit up like a shining Christmas star, or snowflake, Isabel hadn't quite decided—bright white in an inky-black night. Below them the streets of Paris stretched out in all directions, long straight roads of lights, a thin layer of snow on the rooftops as if someone had dusted the city with icing sugar. The tinny sound of a mechanical organ played the tune of 'O' Come All Ye Faithful' somewhere below them. And even though Isabel knew her nose was probably running she couldn't feel it because she was so very, very cold, and she didn't rightly care. She was high above the most beautiful city she'd ever visited, with a gorgeous sexy man at her side. For the first time in a long time she felt light and free and she had a sudden urge to scream out her joy, to release all the emotion knotted in her chest.

But she didn't, of course.

'That down there is the Tuileries Garden.' Sean pointed to the left, his voice raised because the breeze up here was quite strong…like being jabbed with tiny icicles down underneath her collar, on the tips of her ears, onto her cheeks.

'When I was here before we brought a picnic of baguette and cheese and some pretty rough red wine and ate down there. We had a packet of playing cards and spent hours playing black-jack and watching the world go by. Pretty cool. Mind you, it was July, so the temperature was a little different.'

She realised, then, that he hadn't talked much about those long intervening years. The focus of their conversations recently had been so much on their dark shared past and the now, but not on his life. The wheel jerked downwards and she was able to breathe a bit more evenly as the wind dipped. 'Where did you stay when you were here?'

'In a pretty scuddy backpackers' hostel in the fifth *arrondissement*. We couldn't afford much else. We did the cut-down tour of Paris, actually of Europe—mainly exploring cities on foot and on a very strict budget—so we never managed to go *in* to any of the tourist attractions, we just looked at them from the outside. Basic doesn't describe it. We spent a lot of time sleeping rough at train stations and during train journeys, to save money…which we spent, mostly, on beer.'

'I bet it was fun, though.' Intriguing. Carefree. A stab of envy ripped through her gut. 'Daddy always insisted on luxury travel so I've never done anything like that.' This trip had been safe-guarded by a job—but now she felt as if she wanted to spread her wings a little, to live a lit-tle bit more, to move away from that very safe comfort zone she'd erected alongside the emo-tional walls. She wanted to breathe deeply, to fill her lungs with exotic air.

And then there was the question that had been forming on her lips for the last couple of min-utes. 'We?'

He shrugged. 'Yeah. I travelled around with a friend.'

'Girl?'

His eyebrows rose. 'Yes.'

'Er…romantic friend?'

'Yes.'

It was silly to be jealous, and she wasn't really; after all she'd had her share of liaisons. None of them serious, she'd made sure of it…but she'd dabbled. And she couldn't help wanting to learn a little more about Sean's past. How much dabbling had he done? 'What happened to her?' *To your relationship. Your heart.*

'She went back to Brisbane. She's a GP now up on the Sunshine Coast.'

'Was it serious?'

He turned to look fully at her. 'Whoa, so many questions, Isabel. We broke up, a long time ago. So no, clearly it wasn't serious.'

'What happened?'

He looked away then, out over Paris, and she wanted so much to ask him again. *What happened to her? To you?* But then he turned back. 'Apparently I don't trust enough. Or commit… or something.'

'Because of me, what I did to you?' She waved that thought away. Too self-absorbed to think she'd be the reason his relationship had broken up. 'No, forget I said that, way too silly. I didn't mean it.'

'You really want to know?' His eyes blazed. 'Okay. Stacey—my ex—reckoned there was a part of me that was always looking backwards, comparing everyone to you. All that first love angst…yada-yada…'

'Oh. Wow. Really?'

His hand was on her arm now, which he squeezed, almost playfully. 'Of course, that's a whole lot of crock, so don't get any ideas of grandeur. Things just didn't work out. Now, after the day we've had, after what we've just done on the bridge, on a night like this—with the snow and the lights and the laughter everywhere—we are not going to talk about my old doomed relationships.' He shook his head and laughed, but Isabel got the feeling that there was a lot of truth in what he'd said and he was making light of it. That he had been affected by what had happened. Had she really ruined him for any other woman? 'Unless you want me to ask about your past lovers too? A pity fest?'

He had a point. Even though he was making a joke, what they'd shared all those years ago had been very real and raw and if she was honest she had been searching for that connectedness and never found it since. 'No, you really do not need to hear about my shabby love life.'

'Good.' The Ferris-wheel attendant opened the gate and let them out. Once on terra firma Sean shivered and stamped his feet. 'Okay, I'm hungry. You want to find something to eat?'

Isabel indicated the food in her brown paper sacks. 'We could have a picnic?'

He laughed. 'It's probably just about hit zero degrees Celsius. There's no way I'm having a picnic out here. The food will likely freeze, if we don't first.'

'I wasn't talking about outside, you idiot. I was talking about in my room. It's warm and dry and there's wine in the cupboard, Cognac in my bag.'

He took hold of the bags in one hand and wrapped his other round her waist. 'I like your thinking. Mine has a view of the Eiffel Tower. From the main room. Straight across.'

'Yours it is, then. But, Sean...' She rose on her tiptoes.

'Yes?'

'Don't think for a minute that I'm going to pretend that all those years haven't gone by. I want to know what you did. I want to know what you like. I want to know who you are now and what shaped you. I want to know every-thing.' Instead of creating a reality in her head that clearly wasn't true.

'Everything?'

'Everything.'

His grip on her waist tightened as he crushed her against him. She could feel his heat and his strength and she wanted to feel more of it. Pref-erably naked. His voice was rough with desire. 'I can tell you what I like if that helps? Actually… I can show you.'

If he meant what she thought he meant, they needed a taxi, and quick. 'That works for me.'

Within half an hour they were in Sean's room. The view was indeed breathtaking, but she'd come to realise that every view of Paris took her breath away—it was that kind of place: stunning buildings, amazing artworks, sophisticated peo-ple. Was any of it rubbing off on her? Was she becoming that nonchalant Frenchwoman she'd tried to be? She sorely doubted it. But at least some of who she'd been had been stripped away a little. She was starting to feel new, different.

He'd found plates and knives in a drawer,

opened a bottle of Bordeaux and sat in the middle of the bed with food on a blanket and two glasses in his hand. And with far too many clothes on.

Just the wall lights were lit and the way they highlighted the dark curls of his hair and the ridges and shadows of his face made her want to lean in and kiss him. To run her fingers over his face, to explore the new terrain of his features. Breath left her lungs when he raised his head and his dark gaze locked with hers, his intentions very clear now. There was stark hunger in his eyes; desire, thick and tangible, filled the heavy air around them. The strength of her need shocked her. It took all of her resolve not to undress him right there. But this was a day she wanted to remember as much for the loving as the letting go—she wanted to take her time getting to know him properly.

'What are you waiting for, Isabel? You know, I still can't get used to calling you that. You'll be my Izzy for ever.'

Those words gave her a shiver of delight because, more than anything, she wanted to be his Izzy today.

As he lifted his glass to his lips she saw a bare patch of skin on his forearm, a linear scar about three inches long. 'Come sit down. I have wine.'

'You have a scar there. What's that about?'

'This?' He looked down at the place she was pointing to. 'Geez, I can't even remember. Maybe a sports thing? Surfing, maybe? Yeah, probably surfing. I took a bad dunking down at Portsea, which ripped a layer of skin off. Years ago now.'

'You used to love surfing. Sometimes I thought there was no contest—you'd choose that board over me any day.'

'Nah…it was just a teenage obsession. I haven't done it for a while. Not since…' He ran his hand through his hair as he stared at the scar. 'Well, probably not since I did this.'

'Oh, well, I'll kiss it better anyway, seeing as I missed my chance when it happened.' When her lips made contact with his skin she tasted soap and imagined the salt and sunshine taste of the beach. She imagined him wet and bedraggled.

Hot and languid from exercise. At the touch of her tongue on such a tender place he groaned. She smiled and pulled his thick sweater over his head, revealing a navy-blue body-hugging T-shirt. Her fingers trailed down to his hand, where she slid her fingers in between his. 'Any more injuries that need some care and attention from a very dedicated doctor?'

'Hmm…I like where you're going with his.' He levered himself up against the headboard. 'When I was nineteen I was playing Aussie rules footie and broke my wrist.'

'Poor you.' She picked up his left arm and kissed his wrist.

'It was the other one.'

'Oops.'

'Aha.' He slid his hand to the back of her head and pulled her in for a kiss; he tasted of wine and promise, and hot lust coiled through her gut. Her heart was beating hard and fast and the shaking had melded into confidence and daring. His eyes still didn't leave hers. 'When I was twenty-two I broke two left ribs in a motorbike crash.'

'Someone else's bike? No?' She guessed she

must have looked pretty prim, with her mouth wide open at his admission, so she tried to look as if his having a death wish was the most acceptable thing in the world. 'You had a motorbike?'

'When I lived in Sydney, it was a lot cheaper to get around. I loved that motorbike.' His hands pressed under her top, around her waist—bare skin on skin making her shiver with more need—pulling her closer. 'Still do.'

'You have it here? No, surely not.' She crawled across him to straddle his lap; the warmth of his skin stoked her soul, spanning out from her core to her legs, arms, fingers. 'In Cambridge? How do I not know this?'

'Clearly I have a different one in Cambridge, but my old Triumph is waiting for me in Melbourne, at my parents' house.' He cupped her bottom and positioned her over his hardness. 'And why would you know? This is the first time we've really talked about anything in between the last end and the new beginning.'

Getting to know him all over again was very illuminating. Was there nothing about him that didn't excite her? 'Very dangerous. Very edgy… although most people have bicycles in Cambridge. I'd like to see you ride it. In fact, I'd very much like to see you in leathers.'

'I'd like to see you strip them off.' Pulling her top over her head, he palmed her bra, unclipped it, let it fall. 'About those ribs…'

'Oh, yes. Well, clearly this needs to go too.' Naked. She wanted him naked. Without wasting any more time she dragged the T-shirt over his head, exposing his broad, solid chest. She ran her fingers across to his back, skimming over muscles and sinews. Kissed her way from his spine forward to his solar plexus, her tongue taking a detour to his nipples where she sucked one in, making him groan all over again. 'Better?'

'Almost…' His voice raspy and deep. 'When I was twenty-four I had acute appendicitis…'

Giggling, she looked down at his perfect, unblemished abdomen, then back at him. 'You don't have a scar.'

He gave her a wry smile. 'No, it was just a stomach ache in the end, but I think you'd better kiss it better just in case. Just to avoid a flare-up.'

As she licked a trail from nipple to belly button her nipples grazed his jeans. The rough fabric against such sensitive skin made her pause. She was nose to...well, nose to bulge. 'Well, hello, hello... We seem to have a flare-up happening. You...you haven't had any injuries down here?'

'No. All in full working order, ma'am. As I'm sure you remember.'

'I most certainly do.' Thank the good Lord for that. She flicked the button and dragged his jeans off. Took a sharp intake of breath as she looked at him. So supremely sexy. Hard and hot.

'Anything else you want to know? Blood group?'

She knew enough, that he was rhesus negative, because she'd had a Rhesus immunoglobulin injection when she'd had Joshua. But he didn't need to know that. This wasn't the time or the place. 'I want to know...when are you going to kiss me again?'

Then his hands were under her arms, pulling her to face him, his mouth slanting over hers, whispering her name over and over, then fingers plunging into her hair as he kissed her throat, her neck. 'Isabel… *God*, Isabel, the way you make me feel…'

'I know.' Knew what he needed. Another kiss. Touch. The soft silk of skin against skin. The press of heat. Another kiss.

And another. It was in his eyes, in his words, in his voice, in a look. In the beat of his heart against hers. 'Isabel, no more questions…I *know* you now, here.'

'And I *know* you.' She had no care for thinking, for analysing the past, of worrying for the future. She knew him this moment and that was enough.

His teeth grazed her nipples and her head dropped back, her fists in his hair as he feasted. Then his hands moved over her body in a slow teasing study, as if in reverence, down her shoulders, over her breasts, down her belly, slipping to the inside of her thigh.

Oh, God. Yes. She kissed him again full and hard, clutching him closer, and closer still, erasing any space, any past.

'Wait.' He grasped for his jeans and took out a foil, turned onto his side a moment—too long…

she couldn't wait. The ferocity of need stripped her lungs until she gasped for more air, more kisses, more him. He kissed her again and more, and more kisses, wet and greedy, mouths slipping, tongues dancing.

'Sean. I need you.'

'I know, baby. I need you too. So much. So much.' He laid her down and covered her with his body, his hardness so tantalisingly close, his fingers exploring her folds. His thumb skimmed her hard nub and she moaned, opening for him.

'Now, Sean. I need you inside me.'

He slid into her, stretching, filling her so completely it was as if he were made for her. And she gasped again, fitting herself to his rhythm. Her orgasm rising, swelling with each thrust.

'Sean…I…' The rise of emotions thick and full in her chest, she couldn't put them into words.

'I know. I know, Izzy. I know.' This time his kisses were frenzied, hard, rough. And she loved it. Loved his taste and his touch and his scent. Loved the knot of muscles under her fist moving with every thrust. Loved this moment.

Her orgasm shook through her, unbearable and

beautiful in equal measure. His thrusts became faster, deeper, as he too shook as his climax spiralled through him; he was calling her name and clutching her close as if he couldn't bear to ever let her go.

CHAPTER NINE

SEAN WOKE TO bright light filtering through the curtains. Down in the street below there was a siren, voices, the beep of a horn. Paris was awake and, apparently, it thought he should be too. Facing him, curled over onto her side, slept Isabel, blonde hair splayed over the pillow, sheets pulled tightly around her. She looked so peaceful, so rested, so damned perfect that his heart tightened as the questions that had stampeded through his head at midnight played over and over like a stuck record.

Did he want her?

Yes.

Were they rushing things?

Yes.

What did the future hold?

Damned if he knew.

She was everything he'd ever wanted in a

woman—back at school and now—the ideal woman every male wanted to be with. Compassionate. Kind. Beautiful. Sexy. Fun. He'd never been able to believe his luck when she'd chosen him above all the other sixth formers. He could barely believe she was here right now.

Whatever it was that was developing between them was huge. Intense. But she'd broken him once and he'd spent so many years erasing her from his heart, so letting her fully in was causing some trouble. He wanted to. Man, he wanted to, but there was a part of him that just wouldn't let go. Even after yesterday. Such a symbolic and profound moment on the bridge—but that had been about Joshua, not about them. He knew she was scared too and, knowing Isabel, she was a definite flight risk. He couldn't even think about committing to someone who would always be looking over her shoulder and planning when to leave.

Like him, right now.

She reached a hand to his thigh, her voice groggy with sleep. 'Hey there, good morning. Don't even think of going anywhere. I have plans.'

'Me too.' He stroked the underside of her breast. She was so gut-wrenchingly beautiful. 'You wanted to go to see Marina and Teo, and I need to pack if I'm going to get that two o'clock train. Work waits for no man, so I'm told.'

'Do we have five minutes before we start to rush around? Yes, I'd like to see Marina and the boy, but can we just wait a few more moments? I'd like five. Just five.' She curled into his waiting arms and lay there, her breathing calm and steady, oblivious to the turmoil in his head. 'Thank you, Sean, for such a wonderful day yesterday.'

'My pleasure.' And it certainly had been. Just watching her smile had been worth every second. But he wanted more and more and more— and that wanting scared the hell out of him. 'It was a good day all in all.'

'I wish you didn't have to go back. I wish we could stay here like this, warm and cosy and...' she wiggled towards him, her fingers straying upwards along his thigh '...content.'

Content? With a juggernaut of questions steamrollering through his brain? 'How about you ring down for some room-service breakfast? We can have a quick shower, eat and then go?' And maybe with fresh air he'd get some more perspective.

'We can have a shower? Great idea.' Shoving the covers back, she bounded out of bed, then she stopped and looked back at him. 'Come on, what are you waiting for?'

'Just taking in the view...'

'Oh, and you like what you see?' She wiggled her backside at him. Naked. Pretty as a picture. Her long limbs stretching with ease, there were still the vestiges of her last Australian summer there in the fading freckles. Her breasts bobbed slightly as she moved and he remembered how they'd felt under his tongue, how she'd felt astride him.

Apparently perspective was difficult to come by when he was already hard for her again.

What sane man would walk away from this?

'Isabel, I have to leave today.'

The smile fell. 'I know.'

'So we have to talk—'

She came back to him, sat on the duvet and stroked a hand across his bicep. 'No, we don't.'

'Yes.' He anchored her to the bed, hands on her shoulders. 'Stop and listen—'

'No,' she interrupted him, her mouth on his lips now. 'I get it, you know. I totally know that when we leave this room, things will be different. When we go back to work things will be different. So don't go raining on my parade just yet, got it? Give me five damned minutes, that's all I'm asking…give me some of the fairy tale.'

'But—'

Now she'd climbed onto him, straddling his legs—her favourite position, it seemed—pressing herself over his erection. Her lips on his throat. Her glorious heat and wetness on him. Puckered pink nipples pressing against his chest. 'Please, Sean. Don't break the spell… not yet.'

Yes, that was how it felt—as if she'd bewitched him. She kissed him again and his resolve wavered. He cupped her bare cheeks and pulled her closer. The woman wanted five minutes.

Five lifetimes and he'd never have enough of her.

And, what the hell, he was all for a little magic every now and then…

And so she'd taken more than five minutes to savour Sean all over again. *So sue me.* But she'd had to do something to wipe that look from his face—the one that said *I'm sorry, but…*

She hadn't wanted to hear how much he regretted spending these past few days with her or that it had to end because they were going back to work. Or anything other than *let's do it all again.* Because she knew he'd wanted her as much as she'd wanted him—at least, his body had; his brain seemed to be working overtime trying to find problems. And she'd just had to kiss him one more time before the inevitable happened. But the kissing had led to so much more…and now she was in deeper than she'd ever intended.

As they walked up the paediatric ward corridor towards Teo's bed she saw Marina waving at her. She'd showered; her hair was in a neat plait down her back. She was dressed in a hospital gown…and, wait? 'Sean,' Isabel almost screamed as she gripped his arm. 'She's had the baby. Oh, my God, she's had the baby.'

How the heck would Marina cope now?

Isabel dropped her bags, rushed forward and wrapped her new friend into a hug, tussled the grinning boy's hair and then stood back as mum unwrapped the bundle she held tightly in her arms.

'Izzbel…' Marina held the baby out to her, smiling. 'Lucia. Lucia.' And then she garbled something that Isabel didn't understand but she took the sleeping baby from Marina's outstretched hands and held it close. The distinct smell of newborns hit her and her heart melted at once at the tiny snub nose and the dark watchful eyes that seemed to know so much already. She thought about Isla and little Geo and felt a mixture of homesickness and pride. All these babies were true miracles. 'Boy?' She pointed at Sean because the white gown the baby wore gave no hint as to gender. 'Or girl?' She pressed a finger to her own chest, which was thick with joy at this little life, and fear for its future.

Marina pointed at Isabel. *'Fată... Lucia.'*

'Lucia? Her name is Lucia? It must be a girl. Oh, Sean, come and look.' He was sitting down and building bricks with Teo. Just watching him play so gently with the boy made her heart sing. He'd have made a wonderful father, she had no doubt.

She really had to stop berating herself about events of seventeen years ago and start to live for now. She'd promised herself that. She'd even kissed Sean's doubts away long enough to make love with him again, but she couldn't help having a few herself. And being with him brought all those memories to the forefront.

Could they survive the past?

'Sean, come look at this gorgeous girl.'

'Hey there, little one.' He stood and gave Marina a kiss on the cheeks and offered her a very proud smile, but, as with Isabel, there was a question there. What would Marina do now?

Just then, she noticed another woman hovering close by, in a smart straight black skirt and buttoned-up black jacket, dark hair pulled tightly back into a bun. 'Hi. I'm Isabel. I met Marina yesterday at the shelter—we brought her here.'

She didn't smile back. 'Yes, you are Izzbel. Good to meet you. I am Ana, translator.'

'Pleased to meet you. I'm so glad you're here to help.' Isabel nodded, cradling baby Lucia in one arm while she gingerly reached for her bag and brought out the nappies and babygros she'd purchased yesterday. 'Can you please tell Marina I'd like her to have these? And here's some toiletries for her too. Hospital ones are so basic, it's nice to have some luxury.'

Ana did as she was asked. 'Marina says, thank you very much.'

'How is Teo?'

Sean cut in, 'I've just checked through the notes—looks like his fever's settling. Still a bit high, but it's coming down and that's the main thing. He seems chirpier today.'

Isabel brought out the toy fire engine she'd bought for him, leaving the outfits she hadn't been able to resist in the bag. She'd just leave it all here for him rather than have him over-whelmed all at once. 'Here you go, buddy. Here's something for you to play with.'

He took it shyly from her hands and grasped it close to his chest. Marina's eyes pricked with tears as she grabbed Isabel's sleeve and muttered something.

Ana translated in that mechanical voice. 'Again, she says thank you.'

Isabel knew she should probably not ask this question, it was none of her business, but she just couldn't help it. 'Can you tell me, what's the plan for her? Where are they going to be discharged to?'

Ana looked over at Marina, then took Isabel to one side. 'They want to check her for a few days. She has…high blood pressure from the birth—'

'I thought so—pre-eclampsia? They induced her too? That should resolve easily enough, but she has nowhere to live and two small children. It's freezing—'

Ana nodded. 'There is caseworker assigned now. She go to hotel and then to lodging in Éragny when available.'

The baby started to stir and Isabel felt the usual

pull she felt when a baby cried, the ache in her breasts. Her milk had come in after a couple of days and she hadn't known what to do, how to deal with leaks…for the record, tissue stuffed down a bra just made everyone at school think you were trying to impress. She offered Lucia back to her mum. 'I think she might want you.'

Garbling again, Marina shook her head and pushed the baby back to Isabel.

'What's she saying?'

Ana shook her head and looked at the floor. 'She says you can have the girl.' Ana spoke to Marina in the lyrical language, her voice raised. '"Take her," she's saying. "You and your husband can give her better than I can."'

'Husband?' If she wasn't mistaken the look Sean threw her was one of abject horror at the suggestion. Now a different beat began to play in her chest. He didn't want her? Was that it? She wasn't wife material? Did she want to be? She'd never thought about it before…images flashed through her head of a wedding, and smiling Sean and kids…all so inappropriate and yet, so wonderful.

But he didn't want it. And Marina wanted her to be a mother, and Isabel didn't know if she could do that either. Not that she'd ever accept a baby like this, but, well… She walked to Marina and tried to place the baby into her arms. 'No, Marina, take her, please.' It was all becoming just a little too intense. The baby was sniffling now and no doubt preparing to wail for her lunch. And yes, Isabel had material wealth and stability and probably looked like a damned fine bet in Marina's eyes, but she wasn't this baby's mother. And that was what Lucia needed more than anything—her mother's love. Isabel tried to reason with her, lowered her voice and got her eye contact. 'Take your baby, Marina. You're a good mum. Take her.'

Marina shook her head and turned her back as if the deal had been settled.

'Marina, take your baby, please.' Sean's voice had a ring of authority, but was laced with gentleness. He took the infant from Isabel's shaking hands. 'Marina, take your baby. Lucia. Needs. You.'

He handed the baby back to Marina and she

took her with tears streaking her face. She said something very quietly and then turned away again, sat down and started to breastfeed Lucia.

Ana explained, 'She said she had to try. She loves her baby too much to keep her.'

Isabel fought tears of her own. She would not cry. She would subsume this emotion and pretend it didn't exist.

But, oh, it was one thing to have your baby cruelly ripped away because you just couldn't nurture him, another altogether to be willing to hand your child over to strangers in the hope of a happier life. Isabel's heart just about broke into pieces. She sat down next to Marina and stroked her back. 'You'll be okay. You have so much strength and determination. Look at Teo, he's a happy boy chatting away to Sean, he's bonny and—oh, you poor, poor thing. You love her, and that's the most important thing. I'll help you. Somehow.'

Sean was by her side as she looked up; he gave her a soft smile. 'Does this happen a lot? People offering you their babies?'

'No, it's usually a one-way street. I hand the

baby over at delivery—no one's ever offered it back to me.'

'Are you okay?' He ran a thumb down her cheek.

She curled into his touch as his fingers reached her neck. 'I think so.'

'Good.' He pressed a hand to her arm and urged her to stand. 'I think it's best if we leave now. Marina's probably feeling distraught and guilty and...well, I think we've done our best here.'

Isabel shook her head; she wasn't finished. 'I'd like to help her further. Maybe there's a charity I can contact? There must be.'

Ana nodded and gave her a business card. 'We have charities that can help with baby, with childcare and getting Marina job when she is ready. I have network of Romanian people who will help too. Contact me and I give you details.'

'Thank you. So much. I will.' Isabel decided that the formidable Ana would probably not want a hug, so she gave two to Marina instead. Then she kissed little Lucia and knuckled Teo's cheeks gently. If there was one Delamere gene she was proud of it was the determination to help and to make things work out. She would do that for Marina. 'I'll come back soon, I promise. Tomorrow, hopefully.'

Once outside Isabel sucked in a deep breath. 'This was supposed to be just a conference and then some holiday time. I feel wrung out by it all. I think I'm going to need a holiday when I get back to Cambridge.'

Sean's arm was round her shoulder as they walked down the steps and towards the Metro station. 'You take everything to heart, and you shouldn't. She's not your responsibility. Are you like this with all your patients?'

Isabel laughed. 'As if! I'd never get through the day. I manage to keep a perfectly good professional distance but I do care. It's my job to care. But Marina's not my patient. She's…well, she needs a friend, everyone needs that.'

'You don't know anything about her.'

'I know that she loves her kids and that she'd do anything for them. I know that she's desperate and I've been there too.' And he was right, she shouldn't have got involved. But how could she not? Somehow the emotion of the week had got to her.

He'd got to her. Spending time with him had cracked open that barrier she'd so carefully built around her heart and now it seemed she was prey to every emotion out there. That had to stop. And right now.

They'd arrived at the Metro and her heart began its funny little thumping and her tummy began to whirl.

Sean looked at his watch then shrugged a shoulder. 'I'm going to have to go and get that train, but I want to make sure you're all right.'

And now he was going to leave and the moment she'd been dreading reared its ugly head. 'Of course, I'm fine. There are thousands of people like Marina all over the world and I can't help them all. I do understand.'

He pulled her collar around her ears and gave her a look she couldn't read. 'I didn't mean Marina. I meant us. This.'

Us. The thought of it made her hopeful…but then the doubt fairies started to circle again. 'Of course, I'm fine. After I've waved you off with my white handkerchief I'm going to do more shopping…'

He grinned. 'Oh, yes, of course. The deep and meaningful way of dealing with goodbyes.'

'The only way of dealing with anything, surely?' Part of her wanted to cling to his arm and refuse to let him go into the station, to drag him back to bed and replay last night, to never go back to Cambridge or Melbourne and stay here, in Paris, and just be *us*. Her throat was clogged with words she couldn't say to him out loud—the poor guy would run a mile.

But he wasn't going to let it go. 'That's not what I was asking, Isabel.'

Oh, she knew what he was asking, all right, she just didn't know how to answer. 'I mean, it's been really great, Sean, but…geez, husband? I had to chuckle to myself when she said that…'

He frowned. 'That stupid an idea, is it?'

She'd thought he'd have seen the joke too. Thought that the notion of them being married would have made him smile and raise his eyebrows in disbelief. 'What? No. I mean…well…'

His shoulders dropped a little. 'Things will change when we go back to work.'

She infused her voice with fake joy. 'No bed picnics and lie-ins for us…not when we're playing stork and delivering much-wanted babies. Busy on-call rosters. And, besides, in a couple of weeks I'll be heading back to Aussie. You'll be in Cambridge, then who knows where…?'

He nodded. 'You sound as if you're trying to convince yourself that it's not worth the effort.'

'No. That's not it at all.'

He tucked a lock of her hair behind her ear, then his hands skimmed her arms and locked her in place. 'I know you're scared. I understand—it's freaking me out too. So it's probably a good thing that we have this time to take stock. There's a lot to work through.'

'Yes. Of course, so much to think about.'

She thought he was going to walk away but he stepped closer, cupped her face in his hands and brought his mouth close to hers. 'I was angry about what happened, I admit that. I said some stupid things and I apologise. I was a jerk on the train and an idiot at the wine-tasting. It's taken some time for me to get used to the idea of what I missed out on—and it hasn't been easy. Isabel, I'm not a heart-on-my-sleeve kind of bloke, but…it could work, you know. If we wanted it to. We just have to believe. Can you do that?'

The kiss he gave her was lingering and warm. It told her without any doubt that he was willing to do anything to make this work, that he wanted her, that he wanted this.

Did she? *Yes.* Her heart was cheering. Yes.

And still the questions buzzed in her head along with the one true belief she'd kept all those years: *you'll get hurt.*

Plain and simple.

'Can you do that, Izzy? Can you believe?'

Izzy. Oh, yes, in his arms she was Izzy again, she couldn't deny it—he had her down pat. He was the only guy who ever had. But was it enough? She'd done wrong by him and they would never get away from that, from that one night that changed everything. It happened; she couldn't pretend it hadn't. 'I don't know, Sean. I'm sorry.'

He pulled away. 'You need to stop apologising for everything and start to believe in us again.'

She grasped the keys on the chain round her neck. 'I'm going to try. I promise. I'll try.'

'Good. Me too. When are you back in Cambridge?'

'Twenty-third, late...then I'm on call Christmas Eve, dinner at Bonnie's in the evening if I can get away...' She watched him try to keep up and it sounded like a load of excuses, but it was her life—just her life. This was how it was going to be if anything became of *us*—two busy professionals trying to fit each other in—none of the all-consuming togetherness they'd shared here. None of what they'd had all those years ago when life was theirs for the taking. 'I'm at work Christmas Day.'

He pecked a kiss onto her nose and tilted her face up to his. 'I'll see you on Christmas Day then, at work—maybe we can do something after our shifts? I don't want you to be on your own.'

'Thank you, that would be wonderful. I don't want to be alone, either. Dinner, maybe?'

'Yes, dinner. And the rest...everything.' At her

smile he found one too. 'Believe, Izzy. Take a chance.' Then he let her go and turned away, his duffle bag high on his back, taking long, long strides into the busy tube station. And taking, along with him, her heart.

CHAPTER TEN

'OOH, LOVELY, MORE CHOCOLATES!' Isabel reached across the labour suite nurses' station desk and grabbed a chewy toffee from the box before they all disappeared. 'From another grateful client?'

'Hmm, yes.' Bonnie looked up from her seat in front of the computer screen, popped a chocolate into her mouth and sucked; she had a pair of red velvet reindeer ears on a band over her lovely russet-coloured hair. 'It's the best bit about working at Christmas—all the patients get nostalgic about gifts and babies and mangers and we get the benefit. Although there only ever seems to be strawberry creams left when I get to choose.'

'Aww, that's because, as labour suite sister, you make sacrifices for your staff. It's very noble of you.'

Bonnie laughed. 'It's because I'm too busy to stop and eat, more like.'

She did indeed have a busy life, what with a little daughter and now Jacob in her life, plus this unit to run. But, if anyone could make it work, Bonnie could. Isabel felt a wee pang of jealousy—it looked like Sister Bonnie had managed to get it all: family, a man who adored her and a job she loved. Some people really could put their past behind them and believe things could work out. 'Don't worry, sweetie, I'll bring a box of yummy French choccies tonight just for you, specifically with no strawberry creams.'

'Oh, good, are you still coming over for dinner? Freya's so excited to see you—but be warned… Father Christmas is on his way so she'll be hyped-up beyond belief.'

After her now ex-husband's tawdry affair with her best friend, Bonnie had made a fresh start in Cambridge, bringing her daughter away from everything familiar. She had worked hard to make her happy here and to provide everything the girl needed. Isabel had to admit to having fallen just a little bit in love with the little tyke… hyped or not. 'Okay…no worries at all, I'm looking forward to it. Christmas Eve is so special when you're five. How's Jacob bearing up with it all? Must be strange for him to be sharing his house with a ready-made family?'

Bonnie sighed. 'Don't tell him I said so, but he loves it. Underneath that brooding exterior is a sucker for candy canes and Santa sacks. Between you and me he's about as hyped-up as Freya.'

Isabel laughed, imagining their straight-as-a-die, oh-so-professional boss in a Santa outfit. Somehow the image just didn't fit. 'There's a side to him we don't get to see, obviously. I got Freya some gorgeous dresses in Paris...you'll just die when you see them!'

'Oh, that's so sweet, but you know you didn't have to buy her anything, really. Anyway, never mind my terrible twosome, tell me about Dr Dreamcakes. I'm all ears and green with envy. A vacation with him in Paris...' Bonnie put the back of her hand to her forehead and pretended to swoon. 'Naughty Jacob for setting you two up like that. I swear he had an ulterior motive, but he denies all agendas other than a work one. And I'm sorry he couldn't go to Paris with you—that may have been my fault. I wanted to make the build-up to Christmas a special one for Freya, and I put some pressure on Jacob not to go. Still, up close and very personal *à la* France, with a hunk like Sean, what's not to like? How was it?'

Bless her, all loved-up and finally with the full fairy tale, Bonnie hadn't got a clue about the state of Isabel's mind. Her history with Sean had been a well-kept secret from day one and, truth was, Isabel didn't know how it was.

The few extra days in Paris had been filled with thinking and shopping and worrying. And helping Marina, Teo and Lucia move into temporary accommodation. And then there had been a lot more thinking and wishing and panicking about how she really felt. Which was...confused. She'd spent the last few hours at work grateful that Sean had the day off today and that she wouldn't have to face him until tomorrow, because no doubt he'd want some kind of an answer. One more sleepless night to try to sort out her head. 'Oh, you know...it was...Paris.'

'Hey, you're back!' Hope Sanders, one of the other unit midwives, walked out of a side room and wrapped Isabel into a big hug. 'How're you doing? Have you seen the crazy amount of stuff we've got for the first Christmas baby?'

'I know, lucky winner! How on earth they'll get that lot home I don't know. They're going to need to call in Santa and his sleigh.' A huge mountain of gifts now swamped a shopping trolley; the generosity of the unit staff, clients and relatives had been amazing. 'We could halve it and give a prize for the first baby of the new year too.'

'What an excellent idea, Isabel. We could do that and share the love.'

For a moment Isabel thought that her trip might well have been forgotten. Prayed so. Alas no… Hope squeezed a drop of sanitiser onto her hands, rubbed them vigorously and grinned. 'So, come on, how was it? How was Dr Sex-On-Legs? How was Paris? Oh… Wait… Hang on, I've just got to go to the ladies'. Don't say a single word until I get back.'

'Don't worry, I won't…' *Won't say anything at all, if I can help it.* Isabel smiled at her friends. Gosh, she was going to miss this lot when she went home. There was nothing quite like a group of warm and welcoming women to bridge that homesickness gap. They'd all made her very welcome despite their own troubles, and, God knew, they'd all had their fair share over the last year. Bonnie had moved from Scotland and moved in with Jacob before she even knew him; Hope had met and fallen for Aaron, the totally gorgeous American infertility specialist; and rumour had it that midwife Jess Black was also loved up with sexy SCBU doc Dean Edwards, if their spectacular kiss at the Christmas party was anything to go by; but not without a few road bumps along the way for all of them. Somehow they'd survived, the better and happier for it. Apart from Isabel, of course. She was just muddled.

Bonnie smiled as she watched Hope walk down the corridor towards the bathrooms. 'Not that I'm counting, but that's the third time Hope's been to the loo this morning. I hope she's okay. None of my business, of course.'

'No, none whatsoever.' Isabel raised her eyebrows in question, which was girl code for *tell me what you're thinking.*

Bonnie's eyebrows rose in response. 'She seems very happy. Glowing, I'd say.'

'What? D'you think...? No, not Hope...and Aaron? And...pitter-patter?'

'I have no idea...but peeing a lot is one of the first telltale signs...'

Really, nothing was terribly secret on this unit. They all worked long hours and much of their social time was spent together too; they were like family. Everyone knew how gooey Hope went over the newborns, how much she desperately wanted one of her own...and the heat between her and Aaron had been off the scale every time those two had laid eyes on each other. She'd had IVF planned to become a single mum and no one had dared ask her how it had gone; they thought she'd tell them when she had news. Maybe Hope had finally got her dream too?

After a few minutes Isabel watched Hope sauntering back onto the ward, smiling to herself, her hand gently rubbing her abdomen. 'I think if she had anything to tell us she would. It's not for us to speculate.'

Bonnie shrugged and winked. 'All I was saying was that she's spent a lot of time on the loo this morning. And she seems quite happy about it. Nothing gossipy about that, it's all just facts.'

Hope reached them. 'Sorry about that. Now, Isabel, tell me about Paris. Was it wonderful?'

'We had a very interesting conference, thank you.'

'*Interesting?* What exactly does that mean?' Bonnie checked her watch, stood and walked across to Isabel. 'Come on, you can dish the dirt on the way.'

'To lunch? Aww, no, sorry, ladies, much as I'd love to come with you I have so much paperwork to catch up on, emails and stuff, I don't have time today.'

Bonnie's arm looped through Isabel's. 'I thought you'd say that. As it happens we need some extra personnel downstairs…so you're coming with us. We won't keep you too long. I said we'd meet Jess down there.'

'Jess?' Isabel sensed mischief. 'Down where? The cafeteria? I said I can't do lunch. Are we doing lunch?'

'Not so much.' As they strolled towards the

hospital main exit Jess walked towards them, arms full of Santa hats.

'Oh, great, you made it.' Jess gave them all a big grin. Another one in the unit to have had a difficult year, but for whom things were very definitely looking up. 'Thank you so much. I have some extra people coming down from SCBU too, a backing track and some collection boxes. We should make quite a bit, fingers crossed.'

Oh-oh. Isabel felt as if she'd been duped into something she might not enjoy. 'Make what? Doing what?'

'Carol singing.'

'Really? At lunchtime? Why?' *Me? Sing?* 'It's not my thing, really. I have work to do.'

'Oh, come on, sweetheart. You're a long way from home and we thought you might enjoy it.' Bonnie draped some glittery red tinsel over Isabel's shoulder while Jess stuck a red hat on her head. 'Because this is what we do at Christmas. Here's some tinsel—wrap it round your stethoscope. You are going to have a taste of our lovely British traditions. No beach and prawns on the barby…' She put on a terrible Australian accent. 'It's all mince pies, roast chestnuts and lots and lots of singing.'

'We sing. I just don't like doing it all that much.' It was too much of a reminder, all that little baby Jesus stuff. Away in a manger. Lay down his sweet head.

'You'll love it, honestly, and it's for a good cause.' Jess grinned. 'I've even managed to coerce Dean to help out, and that's got to be a first.'

Isabel had had a few professional dealings with Dean Edwards over preemies in SCBU; he was a damned fine doctor and a pretty decent colleague. A bit of a heartthrob too, if she was honest. But no one ever seemed to match up to Sean, no matter how much she looked. And she'd look a heck of a party-pooper if she didn't join in now. Better to get it over with and then leave. 'Dean Edwards, singing? Well, if he's in then I guess I am. I have got to see this.'

'Oh, there he is.' Jess walked towards him as if she were floating on air. She gave him a shy smile and he gave her one in return, oblivious to anyone else in the room. Jess handed him a hat. More *facts* in the department: Jess and Dean were now dating… 'Thank you for coming down.'

Hope stopped mid-tinsel-wrapping. 'Oh…hang on. I just need…wait. I just need to pee. I'll be right back.'

Bonnie threw Isabel a look as if to say *I told you so*, then back at Hope. 'You just went.'

Looking a little sheepish, Hope stuck out her tongue, but the smile stuck. 'Who are you, my mother?'

'Sometimes it feels like I'm everyone's mother here—it comes with the job description.' Bonnie looked at her seriously. 'Hope, are you okay?'

'Yes… Yes, I'm fine. Oh…come here all of you. I need to tell you something.' Hope steered the three of them, Isabel, Jess and Bonnie, across to a quiet corner, took their hands. 'Listen, ladies, this has so got to be a secret, but I can't think straight unless I tell you…I'm pregnant! Sorry, *we're* pregnant, me and Aaron…'

Isabel pretended to look blown away with surprise. 'Wow! That's so fabulous, honey. Well done you. The IVF worked?'

Hope looked as if she was going to burst with excitement. 'No…no, that's just it…I never thought it would happen like this…I went for the implantation and I didn't need it. I was already pregnant. I'm so excited.'

Jess gave her a cuddle and squealed a little. 'Wow, that's just so brilliant. What a Christmas present. You look amazing—feeling okay? No nausea?'

'Not yet. Apart from needing the loo a lot, I'm fine.'

'Okay, yummy mummy, you nip off to the ladies' while we set up. Now, gather round, or we're going to run out of time. I have to get back in twenty minutes.' Jess got them all together into a semicircle by the main doors, in front of a beautiful scented floor-to-ceiling pine Christmas tree, and flicked on the sound system. Handing out sheets of lyrics, she joined them and started to sing 'Away In A Manger'.

Just peachy. As she read through the words Isabel wondered about little Lucia and how she was doing in the new crib that she'd found for her in a Paris baby shop. For some reason the thought of that little scrap of life made her feel a bit heartsore. Or it could have been the excitement of Hope's pregnancy. Or, it could have been, as Sean had suggested, that perhaps she still had that small part inside her that wanted a baby of her own. That perhaps that dream hadn't died along with Joshua after all. Maybe she could open her heart to thinking about that, some time, in the future. She decided as she stood there surrounded by all this love that maybe she would.

As they moved into the second chorus people stopped rushing about and started to listen, and they were smiling and joining in. Beyond the doors the sky was thick and heavy as more snow threatened. Isabel knew that by three-thirty it would be dark outside and that every child in the country would be counting down the hours until that very special jolly man paid them a visit. And so it wouldn't be a swim, then champagne and a barbecue, it wouldn't be sunbathing and lounging around with her family. She'd be here, with this new family of hers, having a very different time, delivering babies and making some people's Christmas a very happy one indeed.

And, as the saying went, a change was as good as a rest.

She watched Hope wipe her eyes as the carol came to an end. The audience had grown quite large and people were generously donating into the buckets at their feet.

Then, at the back of the crowd, she saw a face that sent her heart into overdrive.

He wasn't supposed to be here.

His gaze caught hers and he watched her sing, a small smile on those sensual lips. The world seemed to shrink a little and she felt herself singing the words just to him, and she felt the heat in his gaze. From this distance he probably looked, to everyone else, just like any other guy. But she knew differently.

She knew he was capable of great things, the greatest things anyone could ever do; he was capable of forgiving, of trying to let go, of believing in something that not everyone had the chance to experience in their lives; he was capable of believing in love. With her. He was offering her a chance to have what Hope had, what Jess and Bonnie had, what Isla had, and what everyone deserved: a rich, fulfilling future.

And no, nothing had changed in those last few days, damn it, nothing had changed in those last seventeen years, she still felt gloriously attracted to him; she still craved his touch. Her heart still swelled at the sight of him. She wanted to lean into those shoulders and feel his arms around her; she wanted to lie next to him and talk about the day. She wanted to grow old by his side and somehow make up for the lost years without him. She just had to pluck up the courage to say yes. That was the problem.

After two more songs he gave her a slow wink and walked away.

'What the hell was that about?' Bonnie whispered out of the corner of her mouth as she too watched Sean's back disappear up the corridor. 'What just happened between you two?'

'Shut up and sing.' Isabel smiled through gritted teeth.

And she did. And nothing more was said as

they went through another five carols and raised a couple of hundred pounds for the SCBU.

But later, when just the two of them were walking back to the labour suite, Bonnie stopped and looked straight at Isabel. 'I know it's none of my business—'

'No, it's not.' But she knew her friend had the very best intentions.

'So here are the facts as I see them.' Bonnie smiled gently as heat hit Isabel's cheeks. 'Every time you and Sean are in the same room there are sparks. Tensions soar so high we all feel a need to switch on the fans and get ice. Fact number two: you were heard arguing about your past, about a relationship you had. About lies you told, apparently. And he said he didn't want to see you again. But you went to Paris together. And it was *interesting*.' Another girl-code stare. 'Fact three: the way he looked at you out there just about set the hospital alight. I was torn between decking the halls with boughs of holly and phoning the fire brigade. The man clearly wants you and yet, here you are, looking glum and worried. You want to talk? Because I can listen, very well.'

It would help, Isabel knew, just to say the words out loud. 'Maybe later?'

'Later it'll be Freya and Father Christmas and Jacob and chaos. Trust me, we won't get a chance. I have time now. My office?'

'You hate your office.' Everyone knew that Bonnie never went in there unless she could help it.

'I know, which means no one will find us, so we won't be disturbed.'

Thirty minutes and two cups of strong black coffee later Isabel felt as if she'd bled all over Bonnie's desk. 'So now I have to decide what to do. Take a chance on him, or walk away. I have a plane ticket to Melbourne on New Year's Eve, so essentially I have a week to decide the rest of my life.'

'When are you seeing him again?'

'Tomorrow.'

'So, in reality, you have twenty-four hours.'

'Geez, girlfriend, you are not helping.'

Bonnie shook her head and with a formidable

glint in her eye she leaned forward. Isabel could see why she was a very good match for Jacob— Bonnie would fight for what she wanted, tooth and nail. 'Do you think that if you had a hundred more years to decide it would help? If you love the man you have to take a chance. Do you love him?'

Well, wow, that was a question. She'd tried to put him behind her, she'd tried to erase those feelings, ignored them, subsumed them, but in the end the real question was: had she ever stopped loving him? 'But, Bonnie, how could you dare to let go after what you went through?'

Bonnie's shoulders rose then fell. 'Sometimes you've got to take a risk, and, believe me, I didn't do that lightly. I had Freya to think of. But, well, once I realised I loved him and he loved me I wasn't prepared to let that chance slip through my fingers.' She covered Isabel's hand with her own, and it was almost as if Isla were here talking sense to her. They'd get on well, she thought, her sister and this woman who was fast becoming like one. One day she'd get them to meet, somehow. What a party that would be. 'Come on,

Isabel, I understand what you've been through, but that's all in the past. You have a lot of living to do. What have you got to lose?'

Isabel nodded, fighting the lump in her throat. Bonnie was right, of course—what did she have to lose by loving Sean Anderson? 'Everything. That's the problem.'

'And if he's worth that much to you, you'll take that risk.'

CHAPTER ELEVEN

'ANY ROOM AT the inn?' Johnny, one of the paramedics, breezed into the labour suite, stomping snow from his boots while pushing a young woman on a trolley. For five o'clock in the morning, Christmas Day, the man looked remarkably chipper. The girl, not so.

'Yeah, yeah, very funny. I've never heard that one before. Happy Christmas to you, too.' Sean shook his head and laughed, giving an extra-special smile to the girl on the gurney. She looked so young, pale and frightened. And on her own. Who the hell wanted to be here instead of unwrapping presents? Which was where she should have been right now, with her family looking after her—she barely looked old enough to be out on her own. 'Hello there. Who do we have here?'

The girl gave him a grimace and curled up

around her distended belly. Tears streaked her face as she sucked on portable gas and air. Sean took her in—straggly hair, clothes that were scruffy, long thin bones, skin stretched tight over her cheekbones. Man, she was way too thin.

Johnny handed over a copy of his observation chart. 'This is Phoenix Harding. She's eighteen years old and, we think, about thirty-two weeks pregnant. She's had lower abdominal pain for the past week increasing over time. Lower back pain too. Using gas and air to good effect. Contractions started at around midnight, getting closer together and stronger, every two to three minutes.'

'Okay, thanks, Johnny. We'll take it from here. Hi there, Phoenix, my name's Sean and I'm one of the doctors here. Can you manage to tell me what's been happening?'

She shook her head. Terrified.

'Are you okay if I do some prodding and poking around? I need to have a listen to baby—that will help us work out what to do next.'

She nodded, but hid her face in her hands.

Sean began his assessment, had Hope attach

the heart monitor across Phoenix's belly, and heard a strong quick heartbeat. 'That's sounding good. Baby seems to be quite happy.' But the girl doubled up in pain. He tried to get her to look at him. 'Phoenix, he's not as cooked as we'd like, so we'd prefer to keep him in a little longer. But it looks like he's keen to meet you.'

Phoenix shook her head. Still no words. She looked so young. So frightened. And, as he watched Hope leave the cubicle with an apologetic raise of her eyebrows, in need of a friend and a chaperone.

'Have you got anyone we can call to come and be with you? Friends? Family? Baby's dad?'

Again she shook her head. It was going to be difficult if he had to conduct the assessment by telepathy. 'Hey, missy, just a quick question: can you recall whether your waters broke? It'd have been like a gush of water…an unexpected trickle?'

There was a knock on the door. Isabel stepped into the cubicle and Sean's heart felt as if it were tumbling, mixed with a sharp sense of relief. He never could get used to seeing her without having some kind of reaction. 'Hope's just had to pop out—she thought you'd need a chaperone, everyone else is busy so she asked me to come in.'

After he brought her up to speed with Phoenix's case he added, 'But Phoenix isn't feeling like talking at the moment, so we're taking things slow.'

Isabel nodded, as if she understood exactly what he meant. Thirty-two weeks meant a risk to baby—it was too immature to be born yet. But if it was, they'd need extra care—usually a stint in the SCBU to monitor progress and for special feeding; babies that young often didn't quite get the hang of sucking at a nipple or a teat. Never mind the dangers of immature lungs trying to suck in hospital air.

Isabel smiled at the girl. 'Oh, that's okay, we can take all the time you like, Phoenix.' She paused and stroked the girl's back as she curled into another contraction. 'Although we can't do anything to help if we don't know what's happening. That baby is a bit young to be born yet—so we need to try to keep it in there a bit longer.

Phoenix, do you mind if I examine you?' Time was running out if they wanted to stall the labour; obviously Isabel was fully aware of this.

The girl shook her head and turned onto her back. She looked grateful to have Isabel there at least and when Isabel had done her examination she breathed out a big breath. 'Eight centimetres—wow, you're doing well. And your waters must have broken some time? You don't remember? Can you try to think?'

'No.' Finally a voice.

'Never mind, honey. The main thing is, your cervix is dilating quickly, your baby's on the way. We'll have to give you an injection of steroids to make his lungs good and strong for when he's born. He's going to be a bit small as yet, so we have to give him all the help we can. Is that okay? And I'd like to work out why this is happening now… Have you had any problems or anything over the last few days? Taken any different medicines, drugs? Alcohol? Any accidents, bumps? Done anything really strenuous?'

'No.' As if grabbing onto a life raft Phoenix took hold of the hand Isabel offered to her. 'I've been going to the toilet more. I thought it was just the pregnancy—I read somewhere that you pee more often. But looking back it was twice as many times for half as much wee.'

'In which case we'll need to test your urine as soon as we can. Any fever? Lower back pain?' Isabel reached for a thermometer to continue her assessment.

'Pain, yes.' She pointed to her lumbar region. 'And when I pee.'

'It sounds as if you might have a kidney infection. We'll set up some intravenous antibiotics to help you and to prevent baby getting an infection too.' Isabel inhaled sharply as she helped Phoenix to sit, revealing her skeletal frame under her nightie. 'Have you eaten recently?'

The girl clung to Isabel's arm. 'No, not really. I'm so stupid. I'm so stupid.'

'No, you're not.'

'I should have been more careful. I should have looked after him instead of pretending it wasn't happening.' Then she began to cry thick tears. Isabel held Phoenix as her chest racked with deep sobs for a few minutes. When she'd finished the girl managed to force a few more words out. 'I'm sorry. I'm sorry. I didn't know what to do. I was scared so I didn't tell anyone and I haven't been doing the right things. Have I killed him? Hurt him? Will he be okay?'

'Hey…hush now. We'll sort you out. Don't worry.' Sean watched for Isabel's reaction. It must have been like a rerun of her own life. Which she steadfastly would not allow to interfere here, that much he knew.

She pressed her lips together, took a long deep breath. 'I understand. I do. I know you were scared and that you're scared now. But it will be fine. It will. The main thing is that baby has been growing—clearly. Maybe you'd like a little walk around? Sometimes it's easier if you move.'

Make yourself useful, Sean was telling himself. *Find someone to help her.* 'It's okay. Really, we're here to help. Are you sure you don't want me to phone anyone?'

The girl shook her head vehemently. 'There isn't anyone.'

'There must be someone, surely, sweetheart?'

She was gripping onto Isabel's hand now as pain ripped through her. 'No.'

Damn. Whether there was or wasn't anyone in her life to help her was clearly not up for discussion. 'What are you doing in Cambridge? On your own? Working? Student?'

Phoenix took a deep breath. 'It was supposed to be a fresh start for me and my ex—things hadn't been going well between us in Manchester—he got a job down here so we came. But as soon as he found out about the baby he ran a mile. Or a hundred miles. I have no idea where he is.' She cradled her belly as another contraction rippled through her. When she got through it she asked, her voice weak with fear, 'Have I done something bad to him? Why is he coming so early? I'm not due until March. I can't have him now. I can't.'

Sitting down in the chair next to her, Isabel stroked the girl's arm. 'Sometimes infections can bring on an early labour. All sorts of things can—not eating properly…'

'I was trying to lose weight to hide the bump when I went for job interviews.' Looking de-

7

feated, Phoenix slumped forward. 'It didn't work—I never got any job, I'm starving, he's coming now and I've made a mess of everything.'

'Look, sweetheart, sometimes babies come early. We'll do everything we can to make sure he's okay. But what about you? Have you got any friends to come and help you?'

Their patient shook her head. 'You don't make many friends when you don't go out.'

'What about your midwife? Who did you register with?'

'I didn't. I didn't think. I just wanted it all to go away.' She blinked up at them both with frightened eyes. 'Will you stay with me? And him.'

'Of course we will. Whatever you need, Phoenix.' After giving her the injections Sean stepped forward and took the girl's other hand as another, stronger contraction ripped through her. They were coming thick and fast. No woman should have to face this on her own. 'We'll stay with you, and Hope—the midwife—she'll be back soon and we'll all help you get through this. You'll see.'

Isabel looked across the bed and he felt the punch to his heart as she gave him a weak smile; gratitude shone from her eyes. It gave him some hope for their next conversation. Although there was that nagging sensation again, the one that said she would run as fast as she could, far away from him, all over again. And even though he knew that, the familiar warmth curled through his gut. What was it about her that held him captivated?

He dragged his eyes away from that mass of blonde hair that he loved to run his hands through and turned to listen to Phoenix. Her voice was starting to sound panicked. 'What if I can't do it? What if I'm not strong enough? I'm scared.'

'Don't worry, really. You'll manage. You're young...' He was going to say *and fit and healthy*...but she'd neglected herself a little too much. He had only to hope that the little one had got what it needed from her.

Her body began to tense and she screwed her face up. 'Owwww. I feel like it's pressing down, like I need to push it out. But I don't want to.

He's too little. It's too soon. What if it's…what if he…?'

Isabel gave her a warm smile. 'You're fully dilated now, sweetheart. Your body will work whether you think it's the right time or not, honey. Whatever happens we'll deal with it. You can do this. You can do this.'

But there was a catch in her throat that made Sean lift his head and look at her. She blinked and turned away, shaking her head. Then she turned back, in full control again. 'It's okay, Phoenix. You have me and Sean. We can do this together. Okay? So I need you to breathe like this.'

Isabel began to pant and count.

When Phoenix screamed and bore down, squeezing against Isabel, Sean took over. 'Okay, so breathe with me, Phoenix. Breathe with me. That's a good girl. Lift your legs a little. Well done. I can see the head. Not long to go now.

The girl began to cry. 'Owwww. I don't want to push.'

'You have to push when I say so. Okay? Okay? Okay, Phoenix…you need to push now.' Cradling the head with one hand, he caught the body as it slithered out. He laid it on Phoenix's chest, but she turned away as he cut the cord. Closed her eyes tight shut as tears trickled anyway down her cheeks.

'A girl, you have a daughter, Phoenix.' But the little one wasn't happy to be out in the big wide world. He rubbed her chest with a towel. And again. *Come on. Come on. Breathe for me. Breathe, damn it.*

His gut twisted as he carried her to the Resuscitaire, worked on her until she took a short breath and squawked. A river of relief ran through him. He would not have been able to look at Isabel if this little one hadn't made it. God knew what she was feeling. Dealing with a young desperate teenager and a preemie baby. Although not as preemie as Joshua...

Isabel seemed to have overridden any emotion and was handling the situation with warmth and professionalism; she'd delivered the placenta and was clearing up with a sunny smile. But he could see the stretch in her shoulders, the clench of her jaw. It was costing her a lot to be here, he knew. She'd done that ever since he'd been back in her life again: borne every emotional insult with fastidious grace. She might have called it coping. He called it denial. She refused to be broken. No, she refused to allow anything to reach her emotionally.

'She's beautiful, Phoenix. Do you want to hold her just for a few moments?' He carried the little one over. 'Just hold her against your chest, skin to skin. They love that.'

'No. I don't know what to do. I don't know what to do.' The girl was shaking. 'She's so small. Her skin's too big. She looks…she looks so tiny.'

'Look, she'll love being against your skin.'

She turned away. 'No. I don't…I can't. I'm too scared.'

'It's okay to be scared, sweetheart. But you have the strength to do this. She needs you. She needs her mum.' Isabel cast a worried flicker of her eyes to Sean. This teenager was experiencing the most traumatic experience possibly of her young life—having a premature baby with no emotional support. She needed someone she knew and loved to be with her. 'Hey, are you sure you don't have a friend, your mum, someone who you can at least talk to on the phone? You need someone here for you, Phoenix. You and…your daughter. Have you chosen a name yet?'

'No. I don't know…I thought it was going to be a boy…I thought she was going to die. I thought—'

'Look, she's doing okay. Your daughter is perfect.'

Clearly Phoenix was struggling and needed time to get to grips with all this. And baby needed to be looked after properly—she needed a full assessment, warmth and care. Sean bent to speak to her. 'Okay, so she's managing to breathe fine on her own, she's a trooper, but she's quite little and may not be able to feed properly as yet. I'd like to get her along to the Special Care Baby Unit as soon as we can—get her checked out and warm and looked after. How about I run her along there now and you come with Isabel or Hope when you're a bit more settled?'

Phoenix looked up at Isabel, saw the quick nod of her head. 'Okay. Yes. Okay. Thank you.'

'I'll stay here with Phoenix.' Isabel caught his gaze. She looked as shaken as he felt. He didn't miss the irony—that Isabel had been almost in the same situation, with no one experienced to help her. She'd been through months of worry and anxiety. She hadn't told a soul about her pregnancy. And yet here she was dealing with this.

Her face was fixed in a mask, her emotions hidden so deep that it made his chest ache. Was this how she'd been? Had she shaken like this? Cried? Or had she internalised it all? Damn, he didn't want to think about any of that. Like her, he didn't want to meet those emotions head-on.

But they were there, glittering brightly within him. He wanted to comfort her. He wanted to stroke her worries away. Goddamn, he wanted her, body and soul, more than anything he'd wanted in his whole life.

So, yeah, he loved her. Which was hardly a surprise given that he'd probably been in love with her for most of his life.

Which was a dumb move on his part, because he knew that loving Isabel Delamere was the single most destructive thing he could do. Because she wouldn't allow herself to love him back.

But still, all he wanted to do was take her in his arms and hold her, soothe her pain away. To make her believe how much she meant to him. But he couldn't. He had a professional responsibility to Phoenix and the little scrap of new life in his hands. He also had a responsibility to himself. 'Excellent, I'll see you up there in a little while.' And that would give him a few precious minutes to get his act together too.

CHAPTER TWELVE

HOLD IT IN, Isabel reprimanded herself as she walked to the SCBU. Hopefully he'd have gone by the time she got there. Hopefully she wouldn't see the love in his eyes and feel the need to walk straight into his arms and cry like a baby over things that had happened too long ago. To be held in arms that she still longed to be wrapped inside. To let herself go and love him right back.

No such luck. He was lifting the tiny baby from the incubator; she looked so frail in his strong hands. 'Hi, Isabel. Where's Phoenix?'

'She's having some food and going to have a shower. She's exhausted, poor thing, and over-whelmed.'

'She doesn't want to come?'

Avoiding eye contact, she walked to the baby and gave her a wee stroke on her head. Some-one, one of the nurses, she assumed, had popped a little knitted red Santa hat on her head. It just about broke her heart. 'I think she will. She needs some TLC herself. She's just getting her head around everything. I managed to get a bit of history from her. Basically she has no one. Her mum died a couple of years ago and her dad's been pretty absent for most of her life. There are no siblings. She needs a lot of support. I've warned her about the bells and whistles up here, and the feeding tube and the oxygen. But she's terrified, poor thing.' Then she remembered about the good news she had to tell him. 'But, after all that, she won the first baby of Christmas prize, so at least she's got a few things to tide her over.'

'You don't think she'll decide to put this little one out for adoption?'

'I don't know. She needs a little time to work it all out.'

Cradling the baby in the crook of his arm, he rocked side to side as he spoke. 'How are you?'

'Bearing up, thanks.' She would not break down. She would not let the pain in. And he had no right to look so damned beautiful standing there with a baby in his arms. Her heart thumped with desire, with emotion she did not want to recognise.

'You don't have to hide it from me, you know.' He leaned close enough that, if she'd wanted to, she could have touched him. She could smell his scent, the one that had clung to her body after he'd left her in Paris, and her heart thumped a little more.

She shivered. 'I'm not hiding anything. I'm at work, is all.'

'Isabel, it's been a very emotional morning. You're about at boiling point.'

Thankfully, Dean sauntered over. There was safety in numbers. 'Hey, Happy Christmas!'

'Thanks, you too.'

Dean tickled the baby girl under her chin. 'Is mum coming soon? This little one needs some cuddles.'

'No. She's having a rest.' Grateful for the chance to speak and not to feel Sean's insistent, concerned gaze on her, she filled Dean in on Phoenix's history. 'She's scared stiff and feeling guilty all round, so we need to be gentle with her. I think she'll come round. I'll pop down in an hour or so and see if she wants to come up then.'

'And in the meantime this one needs a cuddle. You want to hold her, Isabel?' He took the baby from Sean and gave her a quick check over. 'Kangaroo care. She really needs some love—especially on Christmas Day. Who doesn't?'

Whoa. Skin-to-skin contact? No. No way was she cradling this baby against her bare skin. That would be the worst thing she could ever do. That would bring back so many memories—she shook her head vehemently. 'No—oh, no, I couldn't.' The little thing was wiggling and her bottom lip had started to shake and Isabel's instinct was to reach out and comfort her, but she couldn't, wouldn't…but, oh, suddenly Dean was helping her to sit and lowering the baby into her arms, onto her chest, which—as bad luck would have it—was covered with a blouse that easily stretched open. She felt the tiny little shudder and curl into her breast, felt the warmth and smelt the just-born fresh scent. For a moment she held her there skin to skin, feeling the life force in this tiny thing, the beating heart where she'd felt none with her own child. And suddenly everything was swimming and blurred from tears she'd steadfastly refused to shed. Ever. It was all too much for her to deal with. The baby. Her memories. Sean. All on Christmas Day. 'I—I just can't.'

And then Sean was there taking the baby and in his eyes he was telling her it was okay, that everything would be okay. He was telling her all the things she'd said to Phoenix. That she was strong enough to deal with it, that she'd be okay.

But she wasn't. She wasn't okay at all. None of this was okay.

'I'm sorry, I think I might…I just…I need to go.' And she hurried out of SCBU, down the stairs and out into the falling snow, trying to force cold air into her lungs.

'Isabel! Izzy, wait. Stop.' It was Sean behind her, his footsteps muffled by the deadening snow. Where it had been beautiful and magical in Paris, now it just felt grey. Ice. The thick air suffocating. 'Isabel.'

She turned. 'I'm going for a walk.'

Warm hands skimmed her arms. 'You have no coat. You're shivering. You shouldn't be out here.'

'Please, Sean, just leave me alone.'

'I can't. I won't.' He caught her up again and pulled her round to face him. 'I know you enough that I feel the pain inside you, Isabel. Talk to me. Let it out.'

If she did she might crumble. She started to walk again, with no idea where she was headed. But the words just tumbled out; she couldn't stop them. 'I used to think it was something I'd done, you know. I thought it was my fault he didn't make it. That I could have saved him if I'd only done…this…or that. But I know he wasn't ever going to make it, Sean. Not like that little one in there. So tiny, so precious and perfect.'

'I understand.'

She came to a halt, whipped round to rail at him. 'Do you? Did you fight against your own body, trying to keep him inside you? To protect him? When you failed at that, did you hold him against your bare chest and sing to him? Did you whisper his name over and over? Did you pray for someone to hold you too? And did you have no one who was capable to take care of you? Oh, yes, Isla was brilliant and so was Evie…but in the end it was me. Just me, and this little life-less thing that I loved with all my heart. And that broke it into tiny pieces that will never ever mend. And just when I had survived and was getting on with my life, just when I was okay, this is reminding me all over again.'

'You will mend and grow again, Isabel. Look at everything you've achieved with your life so far—what an amazing and compassionate doctor you've become. What a beautiful, sensational woman. Just think of what a tour de force we'll be together.' That was a promise from him for the future. He believed in them, that this could work. His arms were round her now and he'd found a bench in the white-coated garden and she was sitting on it and hadn't even noticed. He was warm and safe and for a moment she let him hold her, let him soothe her memories away with a kiss against her throat. He was here, he was making his claim, his stand, his promise and she felt so close to letting go, to believing him. To feeling that everything would turn out fine.

That realisation was enough to jolt her away from him.

She stood. Closed down every emotion, just as she always had, because it was safer that way. Because she had never felt as if her heart had been wrenched from her chest until today—and that surely must mean that she'd allowed herself to get lulled into feeling too much again.

She'd seen him hold a baby, seen the look of contentment on his face, the joy. And she knew she would be unable to commit herself to give him that or anything like it. Ever. Because it couldn't be fine, because she would always be thinking about the worst things that could happen, never giving herself totally to protect herself from breaking into pieces again, and he deserved more than that. So much more.

She'd been too close to the edge just now and she did not want to fall from it. She was too scared, too darned terrified because it would be too hard, so very, very hard to pull herself up from it again. Life had been fine before she'd met Sean again. Empty, but fine. Monochrome, but liveable. She could survive without colour and a full heart and making love, without Paris and without Sean. Without memories and pain and the risk that she could feel so lost again without him. Some time. Once had been enough for any lifetime.

She did not want to bleed for him again. 'I'm so sorry, Sean. I can't do this. *Us.* I'm sorry. There isn't a future and I don't want to let you think there could be.'

'What?' He stood to face her. 'After everything we've been through? You're saying you don't want to try?'

She took a deep breath of the cold, cold air, filled her insides with ice, let it infuse her veins, her blood, because that way she would be able to say these things. 'Yes, that's exactly what I'm saying. It's over, whatever it was, in Paris—whatever I let you believe, I'm sorry.'

But instead of giving the understanding, thoughtful gentle response she expected, he frowned. His voice was laced with anger. 'No, you're not sorry at all. You just want to protect yourself. You want to live a half-life. You want to hide. That's not living, Isabel.'

'Please don't make this harder than it is. It's what I want.'

'And what about what I want? Ever think about that?' When she looked away he huffed out an irritated breath. 'No. I didn't think so.'

'It's not you—' Then she shut up, because all that *it's not you, it's me* gumpf was just a sweetener, and nothing about this was sweet. He had so much to offer, so much promise, so much capability to love—he deserved far more than what she could give him. It made her stomach hurt. It made everything inside her twist and contort and knot. He was right: she hadn't given much thought to how he would be after all this. It had all been about her.

How selfish. How typically Delamere girl. But there it was… She had to do what was right for her; there was no point letting him believe in something that she just couldn't do.

He glared at her. 'Really? You were going to trot out some well-worn phrase? Don't we deserve more than that?' And even though she'd made him cross he was still devastating to look at. His dark eyes still entranced her. There was still that magnetic pull to him that was so hard to resist. She'd been resisting it for too long already. Snow whirled around him like a vortex sticking to his scrubs. He didn't seem to notice. 'You really mean it, don't you? You don't want any of it.'

'No. I don't.'

'You're a coward, Isabel Delamere. You have closed off your life, shut down, checked out. You don't have to bury yourself along with Joshua, you know. You deserve to live.'

'I do live.'

'Hardly. I mean, sure, you get involved with your patients, because that's safe, you know where the line is and you never cross it. You allow yourself to feel their pain, like some sort of proxy for actually feeling things inside you, and then you try to fix them—because you couldn't do that for yourself. But with someone who really cares for you, with me, you totally shut down. You're afraid. I get that, but you have to let people in some time or you'll end up sad and lonely and, well…dead inside.' He pulled her towards him, anger and desire mingling in his eyes. 'I love you. I just think you should know that before I go.'

'Don't—' She put her hand out to his lips, trying to erase his words. 'Don't say that.'

He shrugged her hand away. 'I love you. And I know you love me. I saw it in Paris. I saw it in the way you looked at me. I saw it when we made love. For God's sake, Isabel, don't run away from it this time.'

'No—' She couldn't love him; she'd tried so hard not to. She'd fought and fought to stop him affecting her, to stop him reaching inside her soul and meeting her there, raw and pure. But here she was, out in the snow, having almost lost the plot with him and a preemie and a young girl on Christmas Day. In Paris she'd almost felt that things could be perfect; she'd let them be. She'd almost believed him.

She remembered that feeling at the top of the Ferris wheel—the freedom, the joy of being with him. The way her whole body craved him, and still did now, even more than ever.

And she was struggling to let him go, because she wanted him so much to stay. She did…she did love him.

She closed her eyes against the bitter reality. She loved him totally, utterly…needed him in her life. It was the single worst thing she could do. She hated that she needed him, that she wanted him so much. She hated that they'd become *us* and she couldn't allow herself to be part of that. She'd fallen further under his spell, with his total faith in things working out okay. She needed to go home, to be with Isla—the only person in the world who understood. She needed to put herself back together again.

When she opened her eyes he was closer, his gaze smoky with intent despite the layer of snowflakes in his hair, on his cheeks, on his shoulders. Despite the freezing gale both outside and in her gut. 'Tell me you don't love me and I'll walk away. Tell me, Isabel, that Paris meant nothing to you and I won't stay here another moment.'

'I… What does it matter? I don't want to love you. I can't love you. There it is. Now go, please.'

He stood for a moment, not moving, just looking at her as if willing her to change her mind.

She didn't.

Then he shrugged his shoulders and took one last step towards her. She'd never seen him like this—so coiled and taut, so angry and explosive. And, damn her hormones, she wanted him even more for it. This Sean loved her. This formidable man had been there for her years ago and she hadn't taken him then, this man who had come to find her, who had loved her once, loved her again. It was a second chance.

But he wasn't taking it any more than she could. 'You know what? I'm done chasing you, Isabel. All those years ago you thrashed my heart to pieces because you didn't trust that I would look after you, you couldn't trust me with your secret or your love. All those wasted years we could have been together, exploring the world. Living. Being. Together. That was all I ever wanted from the moment I first saw you in that classroom. And even now, when I've told you again that I love you, you throw it back in my face. Well, that's me done. If you're not willing to take a risk and let me in then I'm gone.' His fingers ran across her throat to the chain that held the keys to his lock. He looked at them, then shook his head. 'I'm finished trying to fight for you, Isabel. I'm finished loving you.'

No. Don't go. She wanted to call to him, to cling to him. To make him stay. He had been her constant. He loved her, still. After everything, he still wanted her. All she had to do was take a step. But she was scared, terrified, so deep-down frozen that she stood there and looked at him. And said nothing.

Don't go. In her head, a tiny voice. *Don't go.* That got louder until it was all she could hear, all she could feel. She clasped the keys on her chain into her fist and tried to swallow through the thick wedge of sadness. *I love you with every beat of my heart.*

But then he swivelled in the snow, stomping long wide footprints back to the hospital entrance, to the happy smiling relatives, to the big sparkling Christmas tree and the jingle-jangle music of Christmas songs. Leaving, in his wake, her frozen body and broken heart.

And only then, when she knew she'd truly lost him, when there was no scrap of hope left, did she crumble to the bench and let the tears fall.

CHAPTER THIRTEEN

HAPPY BLOODY CHRISTMAS?

Yeah, right. Happy bloody life. The growing pressure in Sean's chest almost stopped his breath. He had to get away from her.

It was like Groundhog Day. It was as if he'd gone right back to being seventeen again, only worse because, hell—he'd been forewarned and forearmed, he'd known exactly what she was like and yet he'd loved her anyway.

Fists clenched tight against his sides, Sean walked back into the warmth of the hospital, kept on going past the cafeteria, past the labour suite, past the wards and the cleaners' department, past the delivery bay and out to the street at the other side. Then he ran. Along deserted roads covered in a thickening layer of snow. Past closed shops, further past magnificent colleges and the cathedral and onwards to the river.

Along the footpath he ran past laughing families out throwing snowballs, screeching kids on their new bikes struggling with too-big wheels and too-high seats. He ran past hedges of brambles asleep until spring. Past punts, empty of passengers until summer sun hit the city. Past riverside pubs that murmured with laughter and cheer that he did not feel in any cell in his body, past trees and parks and fields. He ran and then he ran some more.

And eventually, when he no longer had the energy to put one foot in front of the other, he came to a stop.

Goddamnit, he had no clue where he was. 'Isabel.' He shouted her name to the sky, to the empty field, as if she might hear him and look for him. Louder, like a lunatic, like a desperate man. 'Isabel!'

But he wasn't desperate; he'd just made a fatal error in falling in love with someone who didn't know how to do the same. He'd tried, he'd laid his heart on the line and she'd stomped on it again. He'd been so close—they'd been so close—to having it all. And she just didn't want it.

Then he realised he had no breath left and he was doubled over trying to fill his lungs, but all he got were icy vocal cords and a searing hacking cough. He was supposed to be on call. He was supposed to be at the hospital doing his job. Not running to get Isabel out of his system—because she was there, indelibly printed on his heart and it was all pointless. He loved her, for God's sake—how bloody stupid. He loved her, needed her, wanted her more than ever and she couldn't see what a wonderful gift the two of them could be together. And even though he'd known this going in, he'd fooled himself into believing it wouldn't happen. Well, no more. He straightened up, looked at the clear blue sky, emptied of its white load, a thin weak sun. But sun nevertheless. He would go onwards, travel some more. See the world. He would put her behind him, forget Paris and Cambridge and the hope and the love. He would recover from the hurt.

Somehow.

He stamped his feet and began to walk back to work.

* * *

'How's she doing?' Five hours and a couple of less straightforward Christmas deliveries later and Isabel had managed to find some time to visit SCBU again. Better that than to wallow in her own troubles. He was gone from her life— she had a week to endure working on side with him, loving him. Then she'd be home in Melbourne and she could put today behind her.

She would get through this, start her life again. In the meantime she just had to make sure she didn't come face to face with him. The crying had eventually stopped—although she had never known that a person could sob so hard for so long. And after she'd splashed her face with water and drunk two cups of fortifying coffee she'd filled her voice with Christmas cheer and come back to her world. She couldn't leave the hospital, but she could certainly fill her day with people so she wasn't free to face him again alone. She could do this. She could. 'Baby Harding? Is she okay?'

'Absolutely fine.' Dean jerked his thumb towards the incubator and gave a wry smile. 'Mum seems to be taking her time, but she's getting there.'

Dressed in some over-large clothes that Isabel guessed were from the goodwill cupboard, Phoenix was sitting on a chair staring at the cot while her baby gurgled in her incubator kicking her waif-like legs in the air. Poor mite. Both of them. They needed each other and neither of them knew how to go about it. Hoping she could perhaps set them on a path, Isabel crossed the unit and bent down next to Phoenix. 'Hey, there. You made it.'

Phoenix shrugged. 'I couldn't leave her here, not on her own.'

'You did good. Now you can watch over her.' And hopefully feel a mother's need to hold her, some time soon. 'How are you feeling?'

'A bit better.'

Isabel nodded and gave her what she hoped was a reassuring smile. 'That's good, isn't it?'

'Yes. I think so. Hope said she'd speak to a social worker and get me some help.' Phoenix looked at her hands. 'I need it. I'm not sure I can do this on my own. It's a big responsibility—a life. Someone else's.'

'You'll be okay. There are people who can support you. I'll make sure of it.'

But Isabel felt guilt settle on her shoulders. Phoenix had no one. No family, no partner, no one to care for her. She'd thought that she'd been in a similar situation, once, but there had been people there for her if she'd asked. Isla, of course. Her parents, if she'd taken a chance. Sean.

Not any more. The sharp stab in her stomach was startling.

Baby Harding started to stir; her body went rigid as she prepared to bawl. 'I think she needs some company.' Isabel gestured towards Dean, asking if she could pick her up. He nodded and winked.

'Phoenix, is it okay if I pick her up?'

'Sure.'

Isabel bent into the crib and scooped up the little one. This time she would keep her feelings out of it. This time there would be no skin to skin—at least not hers. 'Come here, sweetie.

You want a cuddle?' She cradled the baby in her arm, trying to soothe her. Singing a soft lullaby as Phoenix watched from behind her fringe.

'You see this tube?' Isabel pointed to the naso-gastric tube, managing to keep it together. But, oh, how she wished she didn't keep having that image of Sean in her head—the one where he'd looked at her so angrily and walked away. Where he'd finally, totally, given up on her. 'This is to help with her feeds. She hasn't mastered the art of sucking yet, so she needs a bit of help. If you get a chance, hold her close to your breast so she can smell your milk, try popping the tip of your little finger into her mouth and see if she tries to suck. Oh, and that tube in the crib is just for oxygen, if she needs it. But, as you can hear, her lungs are in pretty good condition.'

As bub wailed Isabel continued to chat, inching closer and closer to Phoenix... 'She's got your hair colouring. Look at all that dark fluff. She's gorgeous.'

Tears filled Phoenix's eyes. 'Why won't she stop crying?'

'I think she needs her mum. Maybe?' Dragging a chair next to Phoenix, she sat, still cradling the baby, grateful to have a distraction from Sean—and a little bit of interest from Phoenix if the flicker in her eyes was anything to go by. 'Have you chosen a name for her yet?'

'I was thinking of Sarah. After my mum.'

'It's a pretty name. For a pretty girl.'

Isabel could see Phoenix's fingers twitching. Then the young mum sat on her hands. Maybe she did want to hold her baby, but didn't know how to ask. Didn't dare. Some people were like that; some people had to be guided and were slow to build their confidence, whereas others dived right in. *Like me,* Isabel thought; ho confidence whatsoever when it came to relationships. And then she tried again to rid her mind of all thoughts of Sean.

But it wasn't working. She couldn't not think of him. Her heart swelled at the memory of his face, of his promises. Then it broke all over again.

Noticing all the staff were busy, Isabel tried her strategy to help Phoenix. 'I don't suppose… No. It's okay. I'll ask someone else…'

'What?' Phoenix sat up straight.

'I need to go to the loo. I don't suppose you'd want to take Sarah for a moment. Just for a moment, mind you. I wouldn't ask…only everyone seems busy with feeds and those poor babies needing extra care…'

Biting her lip, Phoenix gave a little smile. 'I… well, I suppose I could. Try.'

'Oh, thank you. You'd be doing me a huge favour.' Very slowly she handed the baby over. 'I thought I'd be useless at holding them when I first started doing this job, but babies are very easy… Look, just support her head here, and keep that hand under her little tush. Good. That's great. You're a natural, Phoenix.'

The baby began to turn her head towards Phoenix's breast and nuzzled in.

'Oh, she knows you're her mum, all right.' Isabel glanced up at Phoenix's face, trying not to place too much emphasis on this because she didn't want to frighten her, or put pressure on her. Gentle was the way to go. But Phoenix's eyes were glittering with tears again. 'She's so small.'

'But you watch, she'll soon put on weight. Now, just sit tight and I'll be back in a mo.'

As Isabel stood she caught a glimpse of Sean's reflection in the entrance-door glass.

Oh. She sucked in a breath. Wow. It was a physical pain in her heart.

She did not want to see him. Did not. 'I…er… I think I'll stay a minute.'

She could do this. She sat back down.

Phoenix watched her. 'Dr Delamere, are you hiding from Dr Anderson?'

'No. I'm just…well, I'm just trying to…'

'I know it when I see it. I've been doing it for the last seven months. Trouble is, it catches up with you in the end.' The girl grinned and lifted Sarah as evidence. 'There are some things you just can't deny any more.'

'Don't be so clever.' Isabel didn't know if he'd seen her, but he hadn't come into the room.

And Phoenix just wouldn't let it drop. 'So, he's a nice guy. Helpful. Good with his hands…'

She would not discuss her personal life with a patient—that would be absolutely stepping over the line. 'Yes, well, I think you need to focus on Sarah.'

'She's asleep.' Phoenix craned her neck to watch the door.

'Ah, yes…anyway…'

Phoenix turned back and grinned again. 'It's okay, he's going now.'

Relief flooding through her, Isabel breathed out and started to relax. 'Good. Thank you.'

'But if I were you I wouldn't run too far away from him. Sexy guy like that.'

'And none of your business.'

Phoenix raised an eyebrow. 'Just saying…if I had a guy look at me the way he looks at you I'd be walking towards him not hiding in a wing-backed chair. You're lucky to have someone like him looking out for you. You're lucky to have someone, full stop.'

So it turned out that young Phoenix was wise beyond her years—and so very alone. And in stark contrast Isabel could have had everything. He'd been there offering her a future regardless of their past but she'd pushed him away. Again.

How lucky was she to have someone like him

in her life, someone to share everything—good times and bad—to walk with her through whatever life threw their way? How very selfish to wallow in the past and not take a chance on loving someone, and having them love you right back. Just because she was scared. Scared of feeling something…but wasn't she feeling things right now? Despair, mainly. Loss. Broken. As if she'd ripped her own heart out of her chest, because it had all been her doing after all.

Isabel turned and watched him disappear down the corridor. Was he avoiding her too? Did he really not want to see her again?

And it hit her with force that she couldn't bear the thought of not having him in her life. Of not loving him for ever. Because she had, it dawned on her now; she'd loved him her whole life. And it was painful and beautiful and every colourful emotion in between. The joy of it all was that he loved her too.

Isabel glanced at Phoenix, who was now pressing her lips against the baby's chest and murmuring the words to a Christmas song that was playing through the speakers. This girl had been so frightened to love her daughter and now it seemed she had decided to. Just like that. She was going to do it alone and it was going to be hard, but she was taking her first steps along that road. She was brave and strong and everything Isabel could be too—if she let it all in. If she let Sean in. Miracles could happen if you let them. Isabel brushed the rogue tears from her cheeks. Maybe it was her turn for one.

But she couldn't find him. She'd tried the labour suite, the cafeteria, the postnatal ward. She'd popped into Theatre and he wasn't there. Which was probably a good thing because she had no idea what she was going to say to him when she caught up with him.

She wandered along the second-floor corridor with her heart beating too fast, panic setting in, looking in every room—stopping short of calling his name. And then, there, he was calmly ambling along towards her, deep in thought, hands in pockets.

She stopped by the chapel and waited for him to see her, watching his reaction as he slowly came to a halt in front of her. She tried to read his face—but it was a mask. It seemed she wasn't the only one who could hide their feelings. 'Isabel. Hello.'

'Sean.' She didn't know how to begin. What to say.

But he spoke first. 'Phoenix seems to be doing okay.'

So he was keeping it professional. 'Yes. Yes, she's getting there. As am I.'

His forehead crinkled as he frowned. 'Sorry, I don't understand.'

'I wanted to tell you that I do love you. That being with you in Paris was the happiest I've ever been in my life.'

He gave a sharp nod. 'Good to know. Now, I need to go—'

'Wait. Please. Don't go, Sean.'

'Is there any point to this?'

'Yes. Yes, Sean…' Pressing her palms against his chest, she made him stand still—because this was her only chance to say how she felt. Out loud to him. This was the only chance and she was going to grab it—and him and their love, whatever it took. 'I was so scared, so very scared to love you—but it happened anyway. In fact, I don't think I ever stopped loving you all these years. But I didn't know how to let you in. I've spent so long pushing people away, not letting myself feel anything, in case I got hurt… I'm sorry. It's taken some time for me to realise, but I know now that I don't want to live my life without you.'

He shook his head and confirmed all hope was gone. He took her hands in his and she thought he was going to drop them, but he spoke, his voice weary. 'I'm tired, Isabel.'

'It's Izzy.' She squeezed her eyes closed to press back the tears, but this time she just couldn't hold them back. Because she was his Izzy. 'To you.'

'I'm tired, Izzy.'

She opened her eyes, because he'd used her pet name. A flicker of hope bloomed bright in her chest. 'Of me?'

'Of having to fight for you, of having to believe for two people. I'm tired of trying to be that person, the one you trust, the one you choose.

And then you not choosing me anyway. I'm over that. I need a life for me. I can't do this any more.'

Her hands stilled against his heart. It was there, solid and strong. He'd been so strong for them both. 'I trust you.'

'Do you, really? Because I haven't seen any sign of that.' He looked as if he didn't believe her, didn't want to. 'Since when?'

'Since for ever.'

'But I need to see it, you needed to show me instead of bottling everything up inside. I love you, but I won't go through that again. I don't want to.'

So she'd pushed him to the edge and he'd stepped right over. 'I see. So there's no chance…?'

There's a small chance, she thought, because he was still holding her hands.

She gripped his tightly and peered up into his dark eyes that shone with light. 'I know I've been a Delamere disaster to live with, but you've got to understand, I love you with all my heart— and I always will. You, me and Joshua—we were a family, even if just for such a short time, and somewhere along the line I stuffed that up. Big time. I lost you and I don't ever want to lose you again, because that would be too much to bear. You remember those dreams we used to have when we were younger? Those happy, silly dreams that we had a lifetime ahead of us, all the things we could do together? Conquer the world and have fun in the process? I know I lost that—it's taken me all these years to find that again—and you've reawakened it. I know we can do great things, we can be great together. Look at how we helped Teo and Marina...'

'That's charity, Izzy. You can do that on your own.'

'Like hell I can. You give me the confidence to do that. You believe I can do that. You make every day worthwhile—waking up with you is the best gift I've ever had.' She wrapped her fist around the keys on the chain at her throat. 'I want to spend the rest of my life with you. I want to wake up with you every day. So, please, Sean—I love you. I want you in my life. I choose you. Please...don't make me beg.'

His eyes widened. 'Why the hell not?'

She swallowed. 'Really? You want me to beg? Is that how it's going to be?' God knew, she'd really, really stuffed up. 'Okay—if that's what it's going to take—'

'Not on your life. I'm joking.' Sean let his hands slip out of hers and made a decision. It was one he'd been toying with in Paris. One he'd made years ago and one he hoped he'd never have to make again. He could hardly believe what she was saying—but he had to. He had to take the chance. She loved him and wanted him.

And he knew it was early days, that she had a long way to go—but he believed she wanted to walk that journey with him. He reached into his pocket and pulled out the box he'd been carrying with him ever since he'd arrived in Cambridge.

'In that case, Isabel Delamere…' Then he took one of her hands and knelt onto one knee. The look on her face was one of love and joy—and he knew he'd seen that before, in Paris, and he would never tire of seeing it. She loved him. He knew it, he felt it.

'Oh, my God, Sean?'

At that moment the chapel doors opened and out streamed a congregation of smiling people who came to a standstill at what they were witnessing. Great. Now he had an audience.

'Izzy, I know this is soon for you—but I want you to know that I will be here for you, I will walk this road with you. I want nothing more than to be part of your family. I will give you all the time in the world for you to choose whether you want more children to add to it, or if you want our family to be just the two of us. But whatever you decide, I will be by your side. I love you, Izzy. Will you marry me?'

He offered her the ring and his solemn promise.

Her soft green eyes were brimming with tears. 'Is that…is that the ring you gave me when I was sixteen?'

'The very same.'

'You kept it?'

A collective *awww* had him turning his head towards the grins and smiles—everyone seemed to be silently cheering him on.

He was starting to get stage fright. 'I guess I always hoped…one day we'd get to use it.' He took her hand again. 'The wait is killing me… And everyone else?'

A murmur of *yes* rippled around the space.

She laughed, her mouth crumpling. 'Oh, Sean, I couldn't imagine a life more wonderful than being with you.' Then she was pulling him up and in his arms and the congregation gave a cheer and a round of applause. As she pressed her lips to his all the other people melted away and he was alone again with her. Just her. The thought that had come back to him time and again over too many wasted years. Just her. His Izzy.

Something akin to the joy he'd seen on her face roared through him. 'I guess that's a yes?'

'Yes. Yes. Yes! When?' Her arms were round his neck.

'Whoa…someone's keen.'

'I want to start now…I want to be with you from now until for ever.'

'Let's start with today, then. Merry Christmas, Izzy.'

'Oh, yes. A very happy Christmas to you, Sean.' Then she gave him a long lingering kiss that left him in no doubt that this would be the happiest Christmas ever.

EPILOGUE

'I CAN'T BELIEVE it's happening…' Isabel looked out of her old bedroom window at her parents' house down to the manicured garden below. If they weren't quick the flowers would droop in the lovely summer heat. She turned to Isla, who looked so exquisitely beautiful in her long pale lilac silk dress, her hair woven with white flowers, eyes glistening with tears, it made Isabel's heart ache. In fact, her heart hadn't stopped aching—in a good way—for the last three hundred and sixty-four days. 'It's like a fairy tale down there.'

'It's your fairy tale—and we need to get on with it. I love you. I'm so proud of you.' Her sister squeezed her hand; her voice was tender and calm and so not the way Isabel was feeling inside. Calm had left her somewhere around the rehearsal dinner last night when nerves and excitement had taken over. Then sleep had evaded her, not because she was scared—those days were long gone—but because she was just counting down the hours until she could see him again and become Mrs Anderson.

'Okay, let's do this.' Isabel swallowed, inhaled deeply and then walked to the door. Would it be too unbridely to just run down there and jump into his arms? She guessed it probably would.

As she took her father's arm and began to walk up the makeshift petal-strewn aisle behind cute-as-a-button flower girl Cora Elliot, Isabel kept her focus on Sean up ahead waiting for her.

He smiled at her.

He had no idea.

She smiled back, hugging to herself the new secret she'd kept from him for the last two days. And she kept that smile as she nodded to the guests who sighed as she walked by. To Darcie, who had become a firm friend and job-share partner over the last year. The part-time role giving her lots of opportunity to volunteer at the homeless clinic and to raise money for those charities that supported pregnant teenage girls.

And she smiled at Lucas, the dashing man by Darcie's side, who was grinning proudly at his little niece, Cora. Then on to Alessi, who was trying—and failing—to wrestle a wriggling Geo into some sort of quiet. Her gorgeous nephew had taken his first steps recently and was causing every kind of mayhem in their household.

The only piece missing from their day was the staff from Cambridge Royal Maternity Unit, who had been such a huge part of their lives, but they'd had a long email from Bonnie this morning wishing them all the luck in the world; news that Hope's baby had been born, a lovely boy for her and Aaron, and that Jess and Dean were just back from honeymoon with very big smiles. Bonnie and Jacob had some good news of their own—a wedding and adoption plans approved.

Gosh, she missed them all. One day...one day, somehow they'd all be together again, but if not in person they talked regularly over the Internet and their friendships were solid and lasting.

But it was so lovely to be here, sharing this day with these special people she loved, at home in

Melbourne—and since opening her heart out to Sean she had truly never felt so loved in her life.

And then she was there, facing him, in front of the celebrant and surrounded by so much love.

As she said her *I wills* and *I dos* she kept her secret tight inside her.

As her husband kissed her she didn't say a word.

But as the speeches were made and she had to raise a glass she just couldn't hold it in any more. 'Hey, husband of mine, this has been the best day of my life.'

'Mine too. Now chink my glass and drink… they're waiting.' He gave her a kiss and a very sexy wink that had her looking forward to her wedding night at the plush vineyard hideaway they'd booked for a honeymoon.

'I…er…I don't think I should do that.' She leaned in closer, careful not to mess up his dark charcoal suit that made him look very definitely the most handsome man in the world. 'Not for the next nine months or so anyway.'

He looked at her, dark eyes shining. 'What? Really?'

'Yes,' she whispered. 'I'm pregnant. And I have a clean bill of health, all going exactly to plan. Perfect? Yes?'

'Yes, you are, my darling.' Then he kissed her again as if he would never have enough.

When he put her down she clinked his glass and the crowd cheered all over again. But still they didn't share their news…because, well, because some things just needed to be enjoyed in private for a while.

The marquee provided decent shade from the searing summer sunshine, but there was a barbecue and music and later a plan for a trip to the beach. Sean surveyed the mayhem as their friends and family began the informal part of the proceedings. 'A little bit different from last Christmas?'

'And next year will be different again, with a little one.' She patted her tummy, which was as flat as it ever was, but she *knew*…she just knew that everything was going to be fine.

Sean ran his thumb down her cheek and she honestly didn't think it could be possible to be any more happy. But she was, a little more every day, by his side, and now as his wife.

'A baby would be totally perfect, but, Izzy, I don't care where we are or what we do or who we're with, just as long as you and I spend the rest of our lives together.'

'Oh, yes, I promise with all my heart.' She picked up her glass and, one last time, clinked it against his. 'Together. For ever.'

* * * * *

MILLS & BOON®
Large Print Medical

July

A Daddy for Baby Zoe?	Fiona Lowe
A Love Against All Odds	Emily Forbes
Her Playboy's Proposal	Kate Hardy
One Night...with Her Boss	Annie O'Neil
A Mother for His Adopted Son	Lynne Marshall
A Kiss to Change Her Life	Karin Baine

August

His Shock Valentine's Proposal	Amy Ruttan
Craving Her Ex-Army Doc	Amy Ruttan
The Man She Could Never Forget	Meredith Webber
The Nurse Who Stole His Heart	Alison Roberts
Her Holiday Miracle	Joanna Neil
Discovering Dr Riley	Annie Claydon

September

The Socialite's Secret	Carol Marinelli
London's Most Eligible Doctor	Annie O'Neil
Saving Maddie's Baby	Marion Lennox
A Sheikh to Capture Her Heart	Meredith Webber
Breaking All Their Rules	Sue MacKay
One Life-Changing Night	Louisa Heaton